Bella Parker

A Bunch of Heather and Other Poems

Bella Parker

A Bunch of Heather and Other Poems

ISBN/EAN: 9783743393431

Manufactured in Europe, USA, Canada, Australia, Japa

Cover: Foto ©Andreas Hilbeck / pixelio.de

Manufactured and distributed by brebook publishing software (www.brebook.com)

Bella Parker

A Bunch of Heather and Other Poems

A Bunch of Heather

AND

Other Poems.

A BUNCH OF HEATHER

AND

OTHER POEMS.

BY

BELLA PARKER.

𝔅𝔯𝔢𝔠𝔥𝔦𝔫:

D. H. EDWARDS, ADVERTISER OFFICE.

EDINBURGH: JOHN MENZIES & CO.
DUNDEE: GEORGE PETRIE.

1889.

Dedication.

———

TO MY FATHER.

CONTENTS.

A BUNCH OF HEATHER

AND OTHER POEMS.

A Bunch of Heather.

'TWAS but this bunch of heather sent to me
    That made me long once more my home
      to see—
This heather, gathered in my native glen
Beneath the shadow of the rugged Ben.
Friend! think you that the home-folks under
    stand
The joy this gives us in a foreign land?

'Tis but, in sleep, or in day-dreams I see
My Highland home—that place so dear to me ;
The mountain rising in its noble pride,
The white-washed houses on its Southern side,
The noisy streamlet tumbling down the hill,

And entering the loch below the mill.
As thoughts turn to the loch my eyes grow wet;
Its wond'rous beauty I can ne'er forget;
Its summer face I see, of changing hue—
One moment black as night, then radiant blue;
Again I see it as on winter night,
Its waves as mountains high, all foaming white,
Or with the moonlight, like a silver band,
Upon its placid face and pebbly strand.
In Boatman Peter's little skiff once more
I idly rock, or with him pull an oar,
Whilst he, between his lessons in the art
Of rowing, strange old-legends would impart.

There stands the kirk upon the green hillside,
Near by, the manse among the trees doth hide;
Close to the kirk, the inn (where one might buy
Aught from a lamb to postage stamps) doth lie.
A stone's cast off, the schoolhouse rears its head,
Rivalling in learning Oxford, it is said.
The man of "isms" and "ologies" I see,
The children's friend as well as teacher he,
A friend to all the feeble, poor, or old,
To right their wrongs, a champion kind and bold;
A welcome guest was he where'er he went,
His words new charms to every gath'ring lent,

And care and sorrow were forgot awhile
When basking in the sunshine of his smile,
Or listening to his jokes and harmless wit,
His humorous tales, as round the fire we'd sit.

I see the houses on the hillside,' where
The shepherd's evening meal I oft would share;
The milk, the barley scones, the home-made
    cheese—
The finest dainties cannot rival these;
Nor is the greeting by rich friends addressed
Aught like the Highland welcome to a guest.
In fancy by the glowing, bright peat-fire
Again I sit beside some grey-haired sire,
His sun-browned hands clasped on his cromag
    stout;
His faithful dogs upon the floor, tired out;
Whilst round his shieling moaned the wintry
    blast,
He'd talk to me of days and times long past.
The politician of the place once more
1 combat with, as in the days of yore,
And argue on the themes of Church and State,
The news of warfare, and the country's fate;
Whilst by the hearth his gentle sister meek
Would sit and smile, but never dare to speak,—

To contradict would foolish be she knew,
For there was none so clever as " our Hugh."

But as the days of old I thus recall,
My bosom heaves, and burning tear-drops fall;
An exile on a foreign shore I roam,
Far from my dearest friends, my Highland home.
Forgive my tears, dear friend, call me not weak;
Such tears have wet the Saviour's holy cheek ;
And He can sympathise and understand
My longing for a sight of my own land.

Our Darling.

WHERE'S an empty cot in the nursery lone,
      By the window an empty chair,
Upon it a frock and two little shoes,
Which our darling never will wear.

Her doggie looks up with a mournful whine,
And waits for his mistress in vain ;
But the days pass by, and she never comes,
And never will come back again.

The birdies come to the window each day,
And wait, as of old, to be fed ;
But they look in vain for their little friend,
They know not our darling is dead.

There's a little mound in the quiet churchyard—
A mound where the violets grow,
And the daisies white and the cowslips bright,
The flowers our darling loved so.

There's one lamb less on this sorrowful earth,
One less to bear sorrow and pain ;
There's one angel more now in Heaven above—
Our darling we'll meet there again.

A Scottish Sabbath.

THE radiant summer Sabbath morning
    breaks,
Rolls softly back the curtain of the night;
The rugged mountains and the fertile vales
Are bathed in rosy light.

No ring of hammer on the anvil's heard,
The mill is silent and the wheel stands still ;
No ploughboy's whistle, sounding loud and clear,
Is heard upon the hill.

The rustic villagers, in Sabbath dress,
Are streaming forth and winding through the
    glen ;
Women and children, young and old, are there,
Greyhaired and youthful men.

The solemn tolling of the dear old bell,
(Though, doubtless, just a wee thing cracked it
    be)
Sounds sweeter far than grand cathedral chimes
Or music fine to me.

Long have I been an exile from my home—
I've lived in sunny South and distant West;
But in these foreign lands I ever longed
For Scotland's day of rest.

I've worshipped God 'neath India's burning sun,
And in St. Peter's gorgeous church at Rome,
In many a minster old—but none of these
Was like the church at home.

The dear old kirk, with ivy on its walls,
And bonnie streamlet singing past its door,
And quiet churchyard, where friends meet with
        friends
To talk the sermon o'er.

I hear again our dear old pastor's voice
Sounding so sweetly through the house of prayer,
A heavenly radiance on his aged face,
The sunlight on his hair.

I hear again my father lead the Psalms,
The dear familiar tunes come back to me,
Sweet plaintive Martyrs and the Hundred Old,
Elgin and wild Dundee.

I see the old oak pew where mother sat,
Her hand in mine, and Sissie on her knee ;
Now father, mother, Sissie, pastor, all
Have crossed the jasper sea.

This life is full of partings, tears, and grief,
There's nothing in this changeful world can last ;
An everlasting Sabbath we'll enjoy
When change and time are past.

In the Hospital Ward.

THEY told me she was dying, but I could
 not think it true
She smiled a loving welcome as she always used
 to do ;
I thought she could not look so glad if death to
 her were nigh,
For I thought it must be sad to the young and
 fair to die.

She was the fairest cottage-girl in all the country
 side,
I felt as proud as any king when she became my
 bride ;
And she was good as well as fair—a thrifty,
 loving wife ;
We knew no care or sorrow—like a happy dream
 seemed life.

We thought our happiness complete when dar-
    ling baby came,
And how we talked and pondered what should
    be our dear one's name;
We called her "May" because she came upon a
    fair May morn;
She was the wisest, dearest child that surely e'er
    was born.

When she was six months old, one night, as I
    came from the mill,
My young wife met me at the door and whispered,
    "Baby's ill!"
I found her in a fever, tossing wild upon her
    bed;
We watched beside her all that night; by morn
    our May was dead.

We missed our baby, oh! so much—our bonnie
    little May;
My wife grew quieter, sadder, and then weaker
    every day;
The doctor said—"She must have proper food,
    and care and rest,
Let her go to the hospital—for her it will be
    best."

And when I went to see her, I said—" Ah, she's
     mending fast ; "
The nurses shook their heads and said—" She
     can't much longer last ; "
But I could not think it true till my darling said
     to me—
" Yes, Willie, dear, I'm going soon with Christ
     and May to be.

" At first I almost thought it hard to leave you
     lonely here,
I wished then God would spare me till the spring-
     time of the year ;
I longed for flowers upon my grave, and not the
     cold, white snow ;
But all those childish thoughts are gone, for
     Jesus wills it so.

" You've been so good and kind to me, my faith-
     ful Willie, dear.
Farewell ! my love ! cling close to Christ ! He
     will your lone life cheer."
I kissed her cheek, she smiled on me, and then
     was far away ;
I was alone, my wife had gone to join our dar-
     ling May.

Homeward Bound.

I'VE missed her in the morning bright, and
    through the livelong day,
My thoughts so often turned to her when I was
    far away;
Sweet mem'ries of those happy days have oft
    come back to me—
Those happy days I spent with her before I
    crossed the sea.

I kiss the flower she gave me—of flowerets fair,
    the best;
We stood beside the mill-stream as the sun sank
    in the west;
She plucked this little floweret, and she whispered
    —" Dearest Jack,
'Tis all I have to give you; keep it safe till you
    come back."

I took the blue "forget-me-not," and clasped her
    to my heart;
I whispered words of comfort—ah! it was so
    hard to part;
But I was a poor fisher lad, with neither lands
    nor wealth;
I vowed I'd work and win her, for I had strength
    and health.

I went out to the diggings, where I stayed ten
    years or more,
And now I'm sailing home again to dear old
    England's shore;
I see my native town once more, I see her on the
    quay;
I clasp my darling in my arms, for she's been
    true to me.

Building on the Sand.

THE golden summer sunlight shone on fair
    St. Andrews Bay ;
It smiled down on a boy and girl upon the sands
    at play.
A gentle, blue-eyed child was she, with curling
    golden hair ;
A dark-haired, black-eyed boy was he—they
    were a happy pair.

She was the doctor's one ewe lamb ; the rector's
    child was he ;
Their mothers both were laid to rest close by the
    murm'ring sea,
Their fathers had been bosom friends for many,
    many years,
Together they had tasted joy—wept many bitter
    tears.

The summer sunlight brightly shone upon their
　　bairns at play;
The waves came rippling, tumbling in across the
　　peaceful bay;
The children built fair palaces, and castles large
　　and grand,
They gathered shells, and laughed and played
　　among the yellow sand.

"We'll have a house like this, dear Nell—a
　　lovely home 'twill be;
We'll build it near our dear old town, beside the
　　bright blue sea;
We'll live together happy there when you and I
　　are wed;
I wish we both were grown up now"—the dark-
　　eyed Douglas said

　　　　.　　　.　　　.　　　.　　　.

The golden summer sunlight shines on fair St.
　　Andrews Bay;
Alas! it does not now smile down upon the
　　bairns at play;
The dark-eyed Douglas kneels alone upon the
　　hard, cold ground,
With streaming eyes he lays sweet flowers upon
　　a grassy mound.

Beside the old Cathedral walls his little playmate
    lies—
His darling Nell, with golden hair and wondrous
    bright blue eyes.
She's sleeping in God's Acre fair, beside the
    murmuring sea ;
" I shall go to her," Douglas says, " though she
    can't come to me."

"Nell's Saviour I shall learn to love, and then
    we'll meet once more,
We'll meet to part not once again upon a
    heavenly shore ;
Our building here could not endure, 'twas raised
    upon the sand,
But in God's house we'll live for aye, in that far-
    off better land."

Rest in the Lord.

"REST in the Lord!" rang through the old
  room dim,
A sweet voice pealing forth the grand old hymn,
Unconscious that outside the window there
A listener sad stood in the chill night air.

"Rest in the Lord!" fell like a soothing balm
On that tired heart; hushed its unrest to calm,
While from the weary eyes did slowly steal
Long pent-up tears with wondrous power to heal.

"Rest in the Lord!" brought back that happy
  time
When all unknown to him were sin and crime;
The village church where in the choir he sang
That very hymn which through the room now
  rang.

His happy home within the sheltered glen ;
His mother's gentle face he saw again ;
She who had ever loved her erring child ;
Oh ! had he killed her by his ways so wild ?

Or if she lived, would she forgive'him still ?
A longing great for home his heart did fill,
And him with hope the singer did inspire,
"The Lord will give to thee thy heart's desire.".

He turned away, resolved the paths of sin
To leave at once, and a new life begin ;
To rest in God and take Him for his guide,
To be his mother's comfort, joy, and pride.

Th' unconscious singer, in the old room dim,
Might never know the power of that grand hymn ;
But angels heard, and there was joy in heaven
O'er one by God and mother fond forgiven.

The Widower.

I AM alone—the funeral train has passed
    Across the threshold of my lonely cot,
And in the winter sunlight fading fast
My love we've laid to rest, for she is not.

What means that word " alone ?" why aches my
    heart ?
Why com'st thou not, my darling, when I call?
Where art thou gone, what was it made us part?
Jeanie, come back to me, my love, my all !

'Tis fifty years to-day since we were wed ;
I proudly brought thee here, my Jeanie fair ;
And now thou'rt numbered with the silent dead,
Oh, how I long to be beside thee there.

Am I alone ? Is there not One on high ?
Hath He not promised never to forsake ?
Will He not comfort those who to Him cry !
Can He not from me this wild sorrow take ?

" Yea I am with thee," whispers low the voice
Of this dear Friend, so tender, gentle, kind ;
Soon will He make my lonely heart rejoice,
Soon in His home my lost love I shall find.

A Woman, and a Queen.

(James II. killed at the siege of Roxburgh Castle, 1460, A.D.)

THE king was dead! the soldiers stood in
horror and dismay
Around their noble leader, who upon the greensward lay,
Killed by a cannon bursting—their young king
so warlike, brave,
Without a moment's warning hurried to an early
grave.

Into the camp with stately step, and proud
majestic mien,
There came among those stricken men the
newly widowed queen,
And leading by the hand she brought her gentle
little son ;
Those men she sought to comfort as few women
could have done.

"My soldiers, mourn not so," she said, "for it is
    all in vain,
Our tears, our wildest sorrow cannot bring him
    back again.
Rise up and take the castle, for *he* wished you so
    to do ;
My little son is now your king—to him, brave
    men, be true ! "

Fired by her words so noble, they renewed the
    siege that hour,
And soon were in possession of the famous Rox-
    burgh Tower ;
And down through all the ages shall the story
    aye be told,
Of the widowed queen so young and fair, but yet
    so brave and bold.

Called.

Lines on the death of a young officer, killed at Abu Klea.

CALLED by the church bells sounding far
   and wide ;
Called to the Church to make fair May his bride,
Called by her sweet lips, " My own husband,
   dear "—
Words full of music to his listening ear.

Called to the front, his honeymoon scarce o'er ;
Called from his home and his dear native shore ;
Called from his weeping, sorrow-stricken wife ;
Called to take part in fierce and mortal strife.

Called from the battle-field home to the sky ;
Called by his Captain to come up on high ;
Called from fierce turmoil to unceasing rest—
One heart is breaking, but God knoweth best.

Thy Will be Done.

"WHY will be done," I said that summer
    evening
I parted from Jim in the peaceful bay ;
" Thy will be done," I said, and, wildly sobbing,
    I watched him sail away.

"Thy will be done," I said as years rolled
    onward,
And my true love had not come back to me ;
"Thy will be done," I murmured as I wandered
    Beside the moaning sea.

"Thy will be done," I said after the tempest
    Had strewn with dead and wreckage our wild
    coast ;
"Thy will be done," when kneeliug in the moon-
    light
    By him I loved the most.

"Thy will be done, Thou knoweth best, my
    Father,"
  I said, and kissed my love, but could not weep;
I knew 'twas best for him, he looked so happy,
    And smiled as if in sleep.

"Thy will be done," I say when in the evenings
    I think of Jim whilst wand'ring on the shore;
And hope to join him soon in yon blest haven,
    Where the sea shall be no more.

"Thy will be done," echoes across the ages,
    The cry of weary hearts bereaved, opprest;
Ah! which of us can say with *heartfelt* meaning,
    "My Father knoweth best?"

Jack's Letter to the Old Folks at Home.

'TIS Sabbath night, our ship is moored in
    lovely Naples Bay;
The whole day long my thoughts have been with
    loved ones far away;
I pause a moment as I write; I close my eyes,
    and then
This foreign shore doth fade away—I see my
    home again.

I fancy how you all have spent this peaceful
    Sabbath day,
At worship, father, you would pray for "Jack,
    who's far away,"
And you and mother then would go to church
    adown the glen,
And there I know you'd think of me and pray
    for me again.

I think I see you in our pew in the old church
    so fair,
The sunlight, mother, on your face, on father's
    silvery hair;
And sister Annie in the choir, and someone else
    I see,
With merry eyes and auburn hair, who's very
    dear to me.

The service o'er, you wander home beside the
    streamlet clear;
The birds sing loud, the trees are green, glad
    summer time is near;
And Dennis Gray sees Annie home, and one with
    soft eyes black
Comes shyly up and sweetly asks—" When did
    you hear from Jack ?"

Oh, mother dear, I often long to see you all
    again,
To wander with my Kathleen fair adown our
    bonnie glen.
I count the days until again I reach dear Scot-
    land's shore—
The anchor's weighed, so goodbye all; God bless
    you o'er and o'er,

Wilt Thou be Mine?

"I CANNOT clothe thee in rich silks from
  distant foreign lands,
I cannot deck with jewels rare those pretty little
  hands,
I have a heart to offer thee, and little else beside,
But wilt thou come, my bonnie lass, to be my
  own dear bride?

" To care for thee, in storm or calm, my aim in
  life will be ;
These horny hands know how to work, and they
  will work for thee ;
Hard labour will be sweet and light, if thou art
  by my side ;
So wilt thou come, my bonnie lass, to be my own
  dear bride ?

"Thy home will be a white-washed cot among
    the birch trees fair,
With honeysuckle on its walls and roses rich
    and rare,
And, singing to thee all day long, near by a
    stream will glide ;
So wilt thou come, my bonnie lass, to be my own
    dear bride ?

"I'll gather rowan berries red to deck thy coal-
    black hair,
And heather white from mountains high I'll
    bring thee, love, to wear ;
And thou wilt have, my sweetheart fair, a man's
    true love beside ;
So wilt thou come, my bonnie lass, to be my own
    dear bride ? "

"I care not for the silken robes which come from
    foreign lands,
What would a humble lassie do with jewels on
    her hands ?
With you to love and work for me, what can I
    want beside ?
Yes, I will come, my bonnie lad, to be your own
    dear bride."

Marguerite.

*'Tis better to have loved and lost
Than never to have loved at all.*

 STAND within God's Acre fair, close by
the murmuring sea,
Beside a new made grave which holds all dear
on earth to me;
My heart, my hopes lie buried there; the joys,
the sweets of life
Have passed away since that sad day I laid to
rest my wife.

We lived together twenty years, our happiness
complete;
She was beloved by everyone, my darling Mar-
guerite;
She was so gentle, true, and good, as well as
passing fair,
She joyed with me when I was glad, and laughed
away my care.

But God my darling wife did take—two weeks
    ago to-day,
I watched her, bent on charity, go o'er the moor-
    land way ;
She turned and kissed her hand to me as o'er the
    moor she sped ;
I did not see my love again until I found her—
    dead.

The day was cold, the sky looked wild, the wind
    began to blow,
I said, "My darling, don't go out, I'm sure it
    soon will snow."
She smiled, "I must go, Alastair, for poor old
    widow Gray
Will want both food and fire, my dear, if I don't
    go to-day."

The snow came on, the wind shrieked loud across
    the moaning sea,
I watched the clock with anxious eyes—where
    could my loved one be ?
'Twas four o'clock, and she had said that she'd
    be home by two,
I must go forth to meet her now, for dark the
    wild sky grew.

Lost on the moor, I wandered long 'midst snow,
    untrodden, white,
Until the winter moon shone forth with pale and
    ghastly light ;
I found the widow's hut at last, nigh buried in
    the snow,
And heard my wife had left for home more than
    four hours ago.

A stifled groan was all I gave, and then, in awful
    fright,
I staggered blindly forth again into the wintry
    night,
And all night long I sought for her, but sought,
    alas, in vain.
I prayed, "God, give me back my wife," in ac-
    cents wild with pain.

I found her when the weary night at length had
    passed away ;
A smile was on her upturned face as 'midst the
    snow she lay.
I kissed her lips, I called aloud, "My bonnie
    Marguerite,
Speak to me, dearest, once again, just once, my
    wife, so sweet."

D

I stand beside her grave to-day, my heart bowed
    down with care ;
"Oh ! help me, Lord, to bear this blow," is my
    half-uttered prayer ;
And through my blinding tears I say as evening
    shadows fall,
"'Tis better to have loved and lost than never
    loved at all.'

Wee Jim, the Newsboy.

HE was only a ragged laddie,
    So dirty, untutored, and wild,
And yet he was " somebody's darling,"
    A blind woman's only child.

His father had died of a fever
    When Jim was but seven years old,
And ever since then, " to help mother,"
    The evening papers he sold.

And night after night, in all weathers,
    Might be heard his shrill childish cry,
In the busy streets of the city,
    " ' Evenin' Telegraft,' please will ye buy ?"

One night when the new fallen snowflakes
    Were lying so thick on the ground,
A carriage came down the street quickly,
    And its wheels gave no warning sound.

Wee Jim, with his papers, was crossing
  Right over the fleet horses' track,
When, noiseless and swift, they were on him
  Before he had time to start back.

A horrified cry from those near him,
  A moment of suffering sore ;
A strange giddy feeling of sickness,
  And then the poor child knew no more.

When wee Jim awoke he was lying
  In a soft bed so clean and so white,
In a room gay with flowers and pictures—
  A room, oh ! so cheerful and bright.

A gentle-faced lady bent o'er him,
  Smiling sweetly down on the boy ;
He said, " Is this Heaven, please leddy ? "
  And his eyes filled with tears of joy.

She told him how he had been injured,
  Then told him how he had been brought
That night to the ward for the children,
  And laid down in that soft, cosy cot.

Ah ! then he remembered, " Whaur's mither ?
    She'll be wond'rin' sair aboot me ;
An' I ken she'll be awfu' anxious,
    For I said I'd be hame to my tea.

" An' whaur are the ha'pennies I'd earned ?
    The papers I yet had to sell ?
Oh ! I maun gang hame noo, my leddy,
    For I feel again nearly quite well."

" My child, you are not nearly well yet,
    I'll send for your mother, my dear ;"
And the nurse, so patient and gentle,
    Brushed quickly away a bright tear.

Came into the ward his blind mother,
    Slow, guiding herself by the wall ;
" Oh, Jamie, what ails ye my laddie ?"
    Sore weeping she sadly did call.

" Oh ! dinna greet for me, dear mither,
    For I'm no hurt sae very sair ;
But I feel—oh, sae tired an' sleepy,"
    He said as she smoothed his dark hair.

" Oh ! mither, this room is sae bonnie,
   Its wa's wi' fine pictur's are bright ;
An' the flooers are sae sweet an' sae lovely,
   An' the beds are sae saft an' white.

"Dear mither, whan first here I waukened,
   Efter I was hurt on the street,
Oh ! I thocht I was up in heaven,
   An' for very joy I did greet.

Guid nicht, I am noo awfu' sleepy,
   I canna come hame or the morn ; "
They told her that Wee Jim was dying ;
   Her bosom with anguish was torn.

All through the long night she knelt by him ;
   While Jim in delirium did cry
In his shrill voice—now, alas ! weakened—
   " ' Evenin' Telegraft,' please will ye buy ? "

The fair morning sunlight was breaking
   Clear over the hill's snowy brow ;
A lone mother was sobbing wildly—
   Her Wee Jim was in heaven now.

Only.

ONLY a golden curl,
   Cut from a dear little head ;
Only a baby's rattle and ring,
   Tied with a ribbon red.

Only a nursery lone,
   Where a mother sits and weeps ;
Only a tiny flower-decked grave,
   Where a darling baby sleeps.

Only an aching heart,
   Which the world can never fill ;
Only white lips which strive hard to say—
   " Father, it is Thy will."

Only a little child,
   Snatched from this world's pain and care ;
Only an angel in Heaven above,
   Waiting a mother there.

Papa's Little Sweetheart.

MERRY and bright and gay is she,
Papa's little sweetheart, aged three;
What a world of mischief lies
In dimpled mouth and hazel eyes,
And naughty tricks are planned with care
In that baby head with its golden hair.

Very solemn and grave is she,
Papa's little sweetheart, no longer three;
See the demure little girl of eight
Off to school with her books and slate;
Counting the hours till Saturday,
When again she can laugh and play.

Gentle, kind, and thoughtful is she,
Papa's little sweetheart now six times three;
Finished with school, his companion now,
Helping papa as she only knows how;
A fav'rite with all, but dearest to him,
Whose step is now feeble and eyes growing dim.

Timid, shy, and loving is she,
Papa's little sweetheart, just twenty-three ;
What a world of happiness lies
In dimpled mouth and hazel eyes ;
Now some other body's sweetheart is she,
But papa's got a son, so happy is he.

"Blood on my Hands."

A RAILWAYMAN'S STORY.

"THERE'S blood on my hands," he cries, and
    he wrings them the whole day long;
"There's blood on my hands, Oh! God, forgive
    me that terrible wrong;"
And the madman paces his room whilst moaning
    in accents wild;
"There is blood on my hands, Oh! God, the
    blood of my wife and child."

Once he was joyful and gay, as happy as you
    Sir, or I,
His life like a peaceful lake, 'neath a cloudless,
    blue summer sky,
With a loving wife and a child so fair, sir, you
    cannot think
How happy they were till Jim fell a prey to the
    curse of drink.

He was down at the pointsman's box, you see it
    just over here,
'Twas his duty the " Parly " to shunt, to leave
    the main line clear
For the mail which went rattling past with a
    thunder which shook the ground,
Whilst the rocks and forests and hills all seemed
    to echo the sound.

Jim's wife, once so happy and bright, began to
    look heartless and sad,
And their cottage, once clean and neat, a dirty,
    shabby look had ;
No wonder she'd lost heart, poor lass, for night
    after night, from " The Rink,"
Her Jim went staggering home, after spending
    his earnings on drink.

We were mates, so I often went and tried to
    reason with Jim,
I spoke of his sorrowing wife, his example to
    little Tim.
I feared there would be a smash, for I'd seen him
    dazed at his work,
I vowed I'd have to report, though 'twas a duty
    I tried to shirk.

Jim begged for another chance, and promised at
    once to repent,
I thought of his poor wife and child; I, for their
    sakos, sir, did relent.
I saw he strove to do right, his wife looked happy
    again,
And, sir, we were all right glad, for Jim was well
    liked 'mong the men.

His wife was asked to the South to visit her
    friend Mrs Trent;
Things were going so well at home, she took
    little Tim and went;
And Jim looked so smart and bright, as he went
    to see her away,
Oh! why could some warning voice not have
    whispered to her to stay?

When Jim got back to the house he found there
    a very old friend,
Who had come from a distant town the evening
    with them to spend;
He said: "Jim, your house is so dull without
    wee Tim and your lass;
Come, let us go down to the Rink—I know you're
    fond of a glass."

The demon was roused once again, though after
    a glass or two,
Jim left and came down to his box, for he had
    his night's work to do ;
I knew that the man was lost as I watched him,
    not without fear,
Draw the levers the "Parly" to shunt, then signal
    the main line "clear."

We did not meet for a week, for after that night
    I was ill ;
When I got back to work again I found Jim was
    drinking still ;
He looked so haggard and wild, such a sad and
    pitiful sight—
I said, "Jim, does your wife soon return ?" He
    gruffly muttered, " To-night."

I saw him go down to his work, not drunk,
    though he'd had quite enough—
Oh ! sir, had I only known he'd more of the
    poisonous stuff
Down in the pointsman's box ; vain regret is no
    use, but I might
Have prevented, I sometimes think, the work of
    that terrible night.

I'd scarcely been home two hours when I heard
    the " Parly " go past ;
I looked at my watch—she was late, the mail
    would be following fast ;
I felt so uneasy that night, and yet I hardly
    knew why—
There seemed a wail in the wind, an ominous
    look in the sky.

I heard the mail thunder past; in a moment
    there was such a crash—
To my dying day in my ears will ring the sound
    of that smash ;
The ghastly sight that I saw when I ran with a
    light to the spot,
Though years have passed, sir, since then, was
    too awful to be forgot.

I heard the pitiful cries of the dying, wounded,
    and crushed ;
I knelt by some little child whose sweet voice
    was for ever hushed ;
I gazed at the dying and dead, until my eyes,
    sir, grew dim—
'Twas a terrible thought to know that this was
    the work of Jim.

I heard a strange fiendish laugh ; I turned, and,
    lo ! there was Jim ;
He knelt 'midst the ghastly mass beside his
    dead wife and wee Tim.
I saw that his reason had fled as he turned with
    his eyes, strangely wild—
"There's blood on my hands, mate," he cried ;
    "The blood of my wife and child."

Childhood's Days.

I REMEMBER, I remember,
　　Our cottage by the mill,
The noisy streamlet tumbling down
　　The rocky, heathery hill;
And the blue-bells by the wayside,
　　And the foxgloves in the glen—
Oh! the happy, happy days of youth,
　　Will they ne'er come back again?

I remember, I remember,
　　The moor where we did play,
The merry stream where Nell and I
　　Would paidle all the day;
And the horses and the oxen,
　　And my father's collie, Ben—
Oh! the happy, happy days of youth,
　　Will they ne'er come back again?

I remember, I remember,
　The old church on the hill,
The churchyard, with its grassy graves,
　So peaceful and so still ;
The pulpit where the parson talked
　So much of " My brethrén "—
Oh ! the happy, happy days of youth,
　Will they ne'er come back again ?

I remember, I remember,
　The pew where Nell and I
Would sit and through the window watch
　The clouds float o'er the sky ;
And long to be once more at play
　Down in the shady glen—
Oh ! the happy, happy days of youth,
　Will they ne'er come back again ?

I remember, I remember,
　One lovely summer day,
When mother, crying, came and said
　Nell could not come to play ;
But I said, 'She'll come to-morrow,
　And to-day I'll play with Ben "—
Oh ! the happy, happy days of youth,
　Will they ne'er come back again ?

I remember, I remember,
　　How mother came that night,
And led me to the bed where Nell
　　Was lying still and white.
She would not speak to me at all,
　　And would not look at Ben ;
Then I knew the happy days of youth
　　Never could come back again.

I remember, I remember,
　　How in time my grief was stayed,
And how again about the house
　　And on the moor I played.
Ah ! I've had my share of sorrow,
　　And of pleasure, too, since then,
But the happy, happy days of youth
　　Have never come again.

Scatter sunbeams round the children,
　　Try to make their young lives bright ;
Only for a short, short season
　　Things are bathed in rosy light.
Griefs and trials come all too quickly,
　　All too soon they will be men—
Then the happy, happy days of youth
　　Never can come back again.

To my Old Man.

LONG years ago, among the purple heather
   We sat when we were young, my dearest
     Joe,
We climbed the hills and wandered by the
   streamlets—
  Ah! that was years ago.

You talked of love, and whispered low and
   tender
  That I was more than all the world to you;
You vowed, with many kisses and caresses,
  To be a husband true.

We've tasted bitter sorrow oft since then, Joe,
  But through it all you've been the same to
   me;
And you could always, when the cloud was
   darkest,
  A silver lining see.

Our cottage once was full of childish laughter,
　The sweetest music in a mother's ear ;
But those dear voices now are stilled for ever,
　Their sound no more we hear.

Our little ones have all gone home before us,
　But soon, dear Joe, we'll go to join them
　　　　there ;
Oh ! how I long to be within that haven,
　For ever free from care.

The Cradle of Logie.

IN the Indian Prince's presence
　　Down Reid knelt upon one knee;
"Oh! I love your daughter dearly,
　　Will you give her, Prince, to me?"

"She is very young and tender,
　　And your home's so far away,
But I'll give my daughter to you
　　If you from the heart can say

"You will guard her, love her, tend her
　　With a love as strong," he said,
"As a mother's when she watches
　　O'er her infant's cradle bed."

All·this Reid of Logie promised,
　　So the Indian Princess fair
Was, with dowry, by her father
　　Given to the Scotchman's care,

Of the gentle Indian maiden
  Soon the Scotchman tiréd grew,
And a thought of fiendish cruelty
  His vile, wicked mind passed through.

He had promised to defend her
  As a child in cradle bed,
So he'd build a cradle for her,
  Not like child's, of stone instead.

Near his house was built the cradle,
  Hideous prison for his wife ;
There, deprived of food and sunshine,
  Soon was ended her short life.

From the distant land of India
  Sailed across the ocean wide
Spies sent by the Prince to find out
  How fared Logie and his bride.

When to India back they journeyed
  They had no good news to tell ;
And for Reid a fearful hatred
  Did the Prince's bosom swell.

He'd have the revenge he sought for,
   Reid, not knowing spics' report,
Now was sailing o'er the ocean
   To the Indian Prince's Court.

By a noble band of Indians,
   With the proud Prince at their head,
Reid was met; he looked so mournful
   As he told his wife was dead.

"Seize him!" cried the proud Prince loudly;
   Bind him to these horses wild;
Lash them up in four directions;
   I will thus avenge my child."

All in vain Reid's cries for "Mercy;"
   There was no such thing for him;
Loud the Prince laughed as the horses
   Tore him quickly limb from limb.

The Young Missionary.

HE was dying in the desert 'midst the
burning waste of sand,
Dying far away from Scotland, his beloved
native land;
He had only reached the station when wild
fever's fiery breath
Stricken had this faithful servant, and he lay at
point of death.

Kneeling by him was a comrade, friends they'd
been for many years,
Each knew all the other's secrets, all his hopes
and all his fears;
They had come across the ocean, Gospel tidings
glad to bring
To the heathen steeped in darkness, to the sad
and suffering.

Whispered low the patient sufferer, "Soon I
    shall my Saviour see ; .
Hamish, friend, oh ! don't take on so, why, lad,
    do you weep for me ?
Had God willed it, I'd have gladly worked with
    you upon this shore,
And I sometimes have a longing friends and
    home to see once more.

"But Thy will be done, my Father ; Thou art
    more than all to me,
And in that fair, better country all my friends
    again I'll see.
When you next write home, dear Hamish, will
    you give them all my love ;
Tell them that I wish them good-night, till we
    meet again above.

"In my dreams last night, dear Hamish, walked
    I by fair Tummel's side,
With young Katie Stewart, the maiden who was
    soon to be my bride ;
Oh, the waters dancing gaily seemed to know
    and share my joy,
As I talked of love to Katie, love which naught
    could e'er destroy.

"And she's mine for aye, my darling, though
    she'll never be my bride,
On a shore we'll hold sweet converse, fairer far
    than Tummel's side ;
There I'll wait for all my loved ones in that land
    of perfect peace,
So good-night, good-night, dear Hamish, till
    good-nights for ever cease."

Home, Sweet Home.

THE roses clamber wild and free upon the
    white-washed walls,
Their scent is borne upon the breeze as soft the
    twilight falls ;
The sweet notes of a woman's voice through
    lattice window steal,
Singing a joyful song as she prepares the even-
    ing meal.

The light of love is in her eyes, her step is firm
    and strong,
Peace and content are on her face and echo
    through her song ;
Her heart is free from every care, no tears dim
    her bright eyes—
Her home is what all homes might be, an
    "earthly paradise."

A smile lights up her radiant face, a smile of
    welcome sweet,
And to the door she quickly goes her husband
    dear to meet;
His kisses fall upon her lips, and on her golden
    hair—
His new-made bride is queen of wives, the fairest
    of the fair.

Next June the roses bloom again upon the
    cottage walls,
And on a peaceful Sabbath eve the twilight
    softly falls
Upon a pair who reverent kneel beside a cradle
    bed,
Where, pillowed, safe from harm there lies a
    little golden head.

They pray for grace to train aright this treasure
    God hath given,
To guide her in the narrow path that leads at
    last to Heaven;
And, like an angel's whisper soft, there comes
    upon the air—
" Be not afraid, the Lord has heard, and will
    receive your prayer."

Yet once again the roses bloom, the roses sweet
and fair,
But Time has many changes wrought upon that
loving pair ;
Their work is o'er, together now for heavenly
rest they wait,
Whilst eyes, and hands, and feet to them is
their dear daughter Kate.

Jamie's Bible.

IN the twilight some were gathered round
    the glowing, bright camp fires,
'Mong them old and well-tried warriors, grey-
    haired, hardy Highland sires ;
There were also youthful soldiers, eager for
    their first affray,
Longing for the morrow's sunrise to proclaim
    the battle day.

There was one, young Jamie Lindsay, a fond
    widowed mother's pride ;
How she wept, that lonely woman, as she sent
    him from her side—
But she buckled on his broadsword, which his
    soldier sire's had been,
Sent him with a mother's blessing to fight
    bravely for his Queen.

While the soldiers laughed and jested, silent by
    the camp-fire bright
Sat young Jamie, and, with pencil in his Bible,
    did he write :
" If I'm killed to-morrow, fighting, he who finds
    this will he take
This small token to my mother, for a Highland
    comrade's sake ?"

Then he wrote upon the fly-leaf—"Mother,
    darling, all is right ;
I have fought for Queen and country as a High-
    land lad should fight ;
Now I've gone to be with Jesus—all my fighting
    here is o'er,
Mother, I am waiting for you on that peaceful,
    heavenly shore."

Morning broke ; began the battle, fierce it raged
    throughout the day ;
Soon upon the blood-stained greensward many
    dead and dying lay.
Far away a lonely woman prayed to God to
    spare her boy—
Ere his mother's prayer was ended he had tasted
    endless joy.

In that humble Highland cottage, where young
    Jamie had been born,
Sat his agéd mother weeping on a lovely summer
    morn ;
In her hands she held a Bible—dirty, torn, and
    stained with gore ;
How she wept and clasped it to her, as she
    kissed it o'er and o'er.

Ah ! how precious was that treasure, brought
    from a far distant land,
Carried to that lonely mother by a loving
    comrade's hand ;
Though with tears she read his message, yet her
    heart was not so sore,
As she whispered, "Jamie, darling, thou art
    only gone before.

"When I sit alone at even with your Bible on
    my knee,
Once again my soldier husband and my boy
    seem near to me ;
In a few short years at longest we shall meet
    again, my boy—
Meet where there are no more partings, but a
    calm and endless joy."

A Floweret.

WHERE have you come from, floweret
       sweet,
Withered and dying in this back street,
Bruised or spurned by hurrying feet!

Where have you come from, bonnie flower?
Were you plucked from some lady's bower?
Worn by some lover for one short hour?

Where you have come from I cannot say;
Where will you go, sweet floweret, to-day?
Here in the street must you wither away?

Down the street there came a small child
With a pale, thin face, and hair unkempt, wild;
She saw the withered floweret and smiled.

She lifted it up with tenderest care,
Then entered a cellar so dark and bare :
I paused to see what the child would do there.

F

"Mother, here is a flower," she said,
And she laid it down on the rude, hard bed,
Close by the weary sufferer's head.

I saw a smile on the mother's face,
Though tears down her cheeks did each other
    chase,
As she whispered—"Thank you, my little
    Grace."

For more than a week as that way I did pass
I saw the flower in a broken glass,
Tenderly cared for by that little lass.

My Laddies.

"I WILL be a soldier," said Willie,
    As he played with his wooden gun;
"I will fight and kill all the Zulus,
    I think 'twill be jolly fun."

"I will be a sailor," said Johnnie,
    "And sail o'er the beautiful sea;
I will visit those foreign countries
    Which father describes oft to me."

"I will be a preacher," said Jamie,
    "And carry the Gospel news grand,
And our dear Saviour's loving message
    Away to some dark heathen land."

        .   .   .   .   .   .
    .

There's, away in the lonely desert,
    A wooden cross only to tell
Were my soldier Willie lies sleeping,
    My Willie, who fought, oh! so well!

No cross marks the grave of my Johnnie,
    No willow waves over his head ;
In the depths of the ocean he's sleeping
    Till the great sea gives up her dead.

And Jamie, my wee, bonnie laddie,
    For long has been safe in the fold,
Safe from this world's care and sorrow ;
    My darling will never grow old.

Some mothers, with hearts slowly breaking,
    Are listening through the long night
For the falt'ring step of a darling son
    Who has strayed from the path of right.

Though my home is lone I am thankful
    That my darling laddies are safe ;
'Tis hard to part, yet 'tis better far
    Than having a prodigal waif.

The Prodigal's Return.

IN dreams one night I wandered o'er my
    native purple heath;
The birch-clad hills above me rose, the river
    flowed beneath;
And from the windows of my home, that rose-
    embowerèd cot,
A light shone out across the moor to guide me
    to the spot.

The kitchen shutters were unclosed, and as I
    gazed within
I wondered how I could have trod so long the
    paths of sin;
I wondered how I could have left a home so
    sweet and bright,
To wander far down that broad road which leads
    to endless night.

I saw my mother sitting by the peat fire's
    glowing light,
Her face looked pale and worn with care, her
    hair was—oh, so white ;
The Book she loved, the best of Books, lay open
    on her knee ;
Her soft grey eyes looked far away—I knew she
    thought of me.

I woke and said—" I will arise and home to
    mother go ;
God has forgiven and she'll forgive, though I
    have sunk so low.
I cannot give her wealth nor gear, but I for her
    will toil—
Oh ! how I long to tread once more my own dear
    native soil."

The summer sun was setting as I crossed my
    native heath ;
A hazy light lay on the hills, the river sang
    beneath,
The scent of heath and meadow queen was borne
    upon the breeze,
The wind like angels' voices whispered soft
    among the trees.

No light shone forth to welcome me as I drew
    near our cot ;
I sighed, "Alas, has mother dear the prodigal
    forgot ?"
Deep have I sinned, but mother will freely, I
    know, forgive—
In happiness and comfort now shall we together
    live."

No mother came, with careworn face and locks
    of snowy hair,
To kiss me as in days of old—our home was cold
    and bare ;
No roses clambered o'er the walls, for they, like
    her, were dead,
And on the door a board was nailed—"To Let"
    was what I read.

You know now why my hair is white, while I'm
    still in my prime ;
You know why I have come to dwell in this far
    distant clime—
The story of the prodigal I read 'neath India's
    sun ;
You need not wonder that I weep, for I, alas, am
    one.

Benighted.

THE path was rough and slippery, I scarce
    knew where to tread;
The night grew dark, and great black clouds
    were gathering overhead;
I was alone on mountain track, far from the
    haunts of men—
Alone one stormy autumn night in a wild High-
    land glen.

I stumbled down the rocky path, with weary,
    falt'ring feet—
Oh! how I longed some man or boy or even
    child to meet;
But o'er that weary waste of moors and hills
    nought could I see,
Except some timid sheep, that gazed with
    wondering eyes at me.

At length, through deepening gloom, I saw a
    faint, far distant light ;
I hurried on with new-found strength, it was a
    welcome sight—
'Twas but a shepherd's hut I reached, so primi-
    tive and small,
To me it seemed a lovelier place than any
    princely hall.

The door was opened by a maid ; exhausted and
    half dead
I told my tale. " You're welcome, sir, come in,"
    she gently said—
" Father, here is a gentleman, who's been lost
    on the moor ;
We'll do the best we can for you, though we are
    very poor."

The shepherd rose—a glorious type of Scotia's
    sons was he,
Such men as this had followed Bruce, such men
    did Wallace see—
" You're welcome, as my daughter said, our
    humble meal to share,
And for your weary limbs she will a heathy
    couch prepare."

Fair Helen was a lovely maid, her father's hope
    and joy,
Fond love for him shone in her eyes, fond love
    without alloy ;
She was so gentle, modest, meek, as well as
    passing fair,
And she had read and pondered much, and in
    our talk could share.

Some happy hours soon passed away, then I
    retired to rest,
While feelings new and strange to me with wild
    joy filled my breast—
I'd found at last that fair ideal I'd sought for
    everywhere ;
I wondered if fair Helen would consent my home
    to share.

In a Welsh parsonage there dwells a woman
    young and fair,
And she has Helen's bright blue eyes and Helen's
    golden hair ;
And as I kiss my wife, I say—" 'Tis strange that
    I should find
' A perfect woman,' best of gifts, remote from all
    mankind."

Hand in Hand.

HAND in hand, Laidman, we've often stood
   Under the trees where we're standing to-
       day,
Breathing a prayer to the Giver of Good,
   Who has guided us safe on life's stormy way.

Hand in hand, dear, fifty long years ago,
   Together one bright summer eve we stood
       here;
Laidman, you asked me, in words sweet and low,
   If I would come your lone dwelling to cheer.

Then here, hand in hand, we plighted our troth
   Just as the sun sank behind yon green hill;
Life had grown suddenly brighter for both—
   Though poor, yet love would our little home
       fill.

Hand in hand, dear, we our first trouble met,
　　When God took the lamb He lent us away ;
Hand in hand, Laidman, we knelt by our pet,
　　Whilst " Thy will be done " we tried hard to
　　　　say.

When God sent twin boys instead of our one
　　We knelt, hand in hand, by their cribs every
　　　　night ;
Again in the morning, ere work had begun,
　　We prayed for wisdom to train them aright.

But when our laddies had grown big and strong
　　'Twas hard to let them go forth from the
　　　　nest—
The house was so lonely, we mourned for them
　　　　long,
　　And yet we hoped that for them 'twould be
　　　　best.

By our cottage door we stood, hand in hand,
　　Waiting for Donald, our dear soldier son ;
He had bravely fought in a foreign land,
　　And would soon be home, for the fighting was
　　　　done.

Ah ! Laidman, dear, shall we ever forget
  The hour the news came that Donald was
    dead ?
Your faith was still strong, though your eyes
    grew wet,
  As "God has left us yet one child," you said.

When Jim was drowned in the wild Irish Sea,
  And hard thoughts of God did my breaking
    heart fill,
You never chided, but reasoned with me,
  Saying, "God has left us each other still."

Hand in hand, dear, now we're aged and grey,
  Under the trees once again here we stand ;
When death comes upon us, as soon now he may,
  Grant, Lord, we may meet him clasped hand
    in hand.

The Dying Soldier.

NAY, my faithful friend, I'm dying, my life
  is ebbing fast,
I fear that every breath I draw is very near my
  last ;
Oh, will you take a message to those friends I
  love so well,
Far away in bonnie Scotland, in that peaceful
  Highland dell ?

Tell my mother not to weep for me, her wayward, blue-eyed Jim,
Soon we shall meet in yon bright land where no
  tears the eyes can dim ;
And tell her that I prayed each night, and read
  my Bible too
(Although some sneered and mocked at me), for
  she wished me so to do.

Tell my brother Jack to guard her and wipe her
    bitter tears,
For I know she'll mourn and weep for me when
    the bagpipes' notes she hears ;
And tell him when he grows a man ne'er from
    her side to roam,
But to be a keeper of the sheep, and stay with
    her at home.

And now I've but one message more—to her I
    love the best,—
Cut off a golden lock for her when this weary
    head's at rest ;
Say I received my death-wound when the fight
    was raging wild—
'Twill soothe her, knowing how I died, for she's
    a soldier's child.

I almost feel it hard to die just when the battle's
    won,
And you'll be marching home again ere sinks
    to-morrow's sun ;
But Jesus bids my fighting cease, and a soldier
    must obey—
So, farewell, friend, we'll meet again in yon
    bright land far away.

Donald.

OLD Donald was a useful man,
    As round the country with his van
From distant Ballintuim he came—
A household word was Donald's name.

He brought fowls living and fowls dead,
And beef and mutton, cheese and bread;
And for the folks in hall and cot
The " People's Journal," too, he brought.

No matter though the wind blew high,
Or lightning flashed across the sky,
Or snow on hills and moorland lay—
Old Donald never missed a day.

The folks rejoiced to see him pass,
With cheery word for lad or lass;
The gossip of the country side
He brought to them from far and wide.

But sometimes at the inns he'd stay
So long, that when he came away
His horse was wiser far than he—
For Donald somehow couldn't see.

And when the night had passed away,
He'd reach his home at break of day ;
An aching pain within his head,
And from his mind his orders fled.

Then how the people in the glen
Would scold when he came back again
Without their mutton, cheese, or bread !
Whilst he would only scratch his head.

Now, Donald, do you wish to thrive,
And hope a roaring trade to drive?
Drink only Adam's wine—I'll bet
Your orders then you'll ne'er forget.

"At Evening Time there shall be Light."

THE setting sun in crimson light shone on
the glistening snow,
It lighted up the snow-capped peaks, the church
spire far below,
And on the windows of the manse a radiance
bright was cast;
Into a patient suff'rer's room a fading sunbeam
passed.

She felt the sunlight on her face, and brightly,
sweetly smiled;
She was so gentle, good, and fair, the minister's
blind child;
The village folks all loved her, into every heart
she'd crept,
No wonder then that Christmas Eve that men
and women wept.

The minister, with tear-dimmed eyes, sat gazing
    on his child—
" Oh ! God, how can I let her go ?" he sobbed in
    accents wild ;
" Since Jessie's death she's been to me dearer
    than very life—
How can I live all lonely here, with neither
    child nor wife ?"

" Daddy," the little suff'rer said—" Daddy, what
    aileth thee ?
Those are not teardrops on my hands !   Daddy,
    don't cry for me ;
Remember we are always glad and gay on
    Christmas Eve—
On this, my last one here on earth, let nothing
    us two grieve.

" As dear old John, the colporteur, to-day was
    passing nigh,
Nurse asked him to come in, because I wished
    to say ' Good-bye ?'
We had a nice talk, Daddy dear, and then I
    asked old John
If he would come and comfort you when little
    Gertie's gone.

" Daddy, there is a lovely verse ('twas meant, I
    think, for me),
I've thought about since I was ill, 'tis this—
    ' Thine eyes shall see ;'
And then there is another, 'twill, I feel, come
    true to-night—
' At evening time,' yea, very soon, for me ' there
    shall be light.'

" I shall not look on earthly scenes, though
    lovely they must be ;
A fairer land and Christ its King in beauty I
    shall see—
Please kiss me, Daddy, once again—there, now
    I'll say good-night."
A stricken father knelt alone ; at even it *was*
    light.

A Tale of War.

THE evening sunbeams brightly fell across
    the sanded floor ;
Two merry children laughed and played beside
    the cottage door ;
The mother in the kitchen clean set out the
    evening meal,
And shuddered as she frequent heard the distant
    cannon peal.

And while she worked she constant prayed—
    "Oh ! God, take care of Jim ;
I've lent him to our noble king, but safe back
    · bring Thou him—
For I could not live without him, my darling
    husband true."
Again she shuddered as the sounds of battle
    louder grew,

The moon rose o'er the mountains; the two
    children were asleep,
The mother, kneeling, prayed to God her Jim
    from harm to keep;
When, hark! amid the tumult of the distant
    cannon's roar,
She heard the heavy tramp of feet come to the
    cottage door.

Four soldiers slowly entered, and a burden sad
    they bore—
A lifeless, gallant soldier, dust-stained and
    steeped in gore;
In broken tones they told her how her Jim had
    fought so well,
And how King James himself had gone and
    raised him when he fell.

Then spake a grey-haired veteran as the tears
    streamed down his face—
"Your husband now is happy in a better, holier
    place,
You must not mourn for him as dead, his life
    has just begun;
Our God will be your stay. Oh! try to say,
    "His will be done.""

Then each man kissed the fair young face of
    their dead soldier friend,
And sadly back to camp again their way they
    slow did wend ;
And she was left to battle with grief women
    only know   ,
When they have loved and lost their dearest,
    best friend here below.

There, kneeling by that silent form, with only
    God to see,
She prayed for strength the blow to bear—God
    gave the victory ;
She rose and kissed his bonnie face, and then his
    broken sword—
" I lent him to his King, now I resign him to
    his Lord."

Is Life Worth Living?

"IS LIFE worth living?" smiles the happy
      bride,
  Leaning her head upon her husband's breast;
"Yes, life is full, so full, of joy to me,
    For I am strangely blest."

"Is life worth living?" moans the suff'ring one,
  Tossing from side to side on bed of pain;
"Life has lost all its sweets for me, and now
     To me ' to die is gain.'"

"Is life worth living?" weeps the mourner said,
  Bereft of husband, father, brother, son;
"Why does God take my all and leave me here?
  Oh! would my life were done!"

Is life worth living? when the stricken heart
  Has been by kindly Time revived and healed?
She says—"In God's own blessèd way He has
  His love to me revealed.

" He knew an earthly love possessed my heart,
    And so He cast my idol to the ground ;
Helpless I turned to Him when life grew dark,
    And comfort sweet I found."

Is life worth living ?   Oh ! it ʻall depends
    On how we spend our time of sojourn here ;
Whether we live and act for self alone,
    Or others strive to cheer.

Our time and money, influence, life itself,
    Were given us by that wondrous One in
        Three,
And He will come one day and say to each—
    " What have you done for Me ?

" Have you passed hours in careless gaiety,
    And days in idle indolence and ease ?
Has precious time been spent in the hard task
    Of trying self to please ?

        .

" Your money have you spent on self alone
    In costly pleasures, food and raiment fine ?
Whilst thousands go in rags, want even bread ;
    And these, the poor, are Mine.

"Or have you tried some lonely life to cheer?
    Some breaking heart to comfort, bind up, heal?
Some fallen one to raise, and My great love
    To sinners to reveal?

"If so, life should be full of joy to you,
    For you are Mine through all eternity;
For what you've done to others, blessèd ones,
    You've also done to Me."

"Lead, Kindly Light, amid the Encircling Gloom."

THEY tell me I must leave my home and all
    my friends so dear;
That I must give up *all* for God without a sigh
    or tear;
That I must spend the rest of life in some
    secluded cell;
That this is what the good monks do, who love
    their dear church well.

They tell me I must quench this love that fills
    with joy my heart,
That darling Violet and I must now for ever
    part;
They say I must to God give up my life, my
    lands, my gold—
Surely the way is not so rough to the Good
    Shepherd's fold.

God is a father kind, I've read in Book of Books
    the best ;
He cannot love to see His sons by doubt and
    woe oppressed,
He cannot wish that we should have no earthly
    loves or joys ;
God planted love in Adam's breast—His works
    He ne'er destroys.

Oh ! must I leave my mother dear, now she is
    lone and weak ?
My mother, who taught me to pray ere I could
    plainly speak ;
Must I my Violet give up ?   We've loved for
    many years—
The monks say—"Son, will you be kept from
    God by women's tears ?"

Oh ! Father give me light, I pray ; 'tis dark, so
    dark around ;
The path is rough, a mist of doubt and fears do
    me confound ;
I cannot see the way to tread—oh ! help me,
    gracious Lord,
Surround me by the holy light of Thy most
    blessed word,

The light has come; the way is plain before my
    new-found sight;
God has upon my darkened soul shed down a
    glorious light.
Thank God, He wills not I for Him my home and
    friends should leave;
I need not break my darling's heart, my pious
    mother grieve.

Maggie.

AN HOSPITAL INCIDENT.

BRUISED and mangled, crushed and bleed-
 ing,
 To the Children's Ward they brought
Maggie Milne, the little weaver,
 Laid her in a soft, white cot,

And the doctors, when they saw her,
 Shook their heads and turned away;
"Nurse," they said, "she'll be in Heaven
 Ere the breaking of the day."

Then the gentle nurse bent o'er her,
 Kissed her little, thin, white face;
"Maggie, dear," she said, "you're going
 To a happy, lovely place,

"Where there is no pain or sorrow—
 All is bright and pure and fair;
Jesus Christ is waiting, Maggie,
 To receive you over there."

" At the Sabbath School, dear lady,
   I have heard of God and Heaven,
And of Jesus Christ, the Saviour,
   Who for sinners lost was given.

" And, dear nurse, I love the Sáviour,
   And I long to go to Him ;
For my mother is in Heaven,
   And my baby brother, Jim.

" But I fear He'll never find me
   'Mong so many in this room ;
Oft I asked Him to come for me,
   While I stood beside the loom,

" For I'd tied a bit of ribbon
   On the loom that He might know
Which was Maggie Milne, the weaver,
   For I longed so much to go."

" Here's some ribbon, I will tie it
   On your cot, and then the Lord
Will know which is little Maggie,
   When he passes through the ward."

"Thank you nurse," the child said gently,
    And a smile of sweet content
Passed across her pale, worn features,
    To her face a glory lent.

Through the ward, when all was silent,
    Softly a bright angel sped ;
Paused beside the cot with ribbon,
    And the child to Heaven led.

Memories of the Past.

SEE him in his garden as I saw him long
ago,
That garden which to me still seems the best on
earth below,
Where the roses and the pansies in their gaudy
hues did vie
With the radiant, dazzling azure of the cloudless
summer sky.

The western wind steals softly through the
overhanging trees,
'Neath which I see him seated, watching earnestly
his bees,
Whilst the partner of his sorrows and his joys
for many a year
In an arbour, with her knitting, sits beside her
husband dear.

II

Down the garden, humming gaily, tripping at a
    rapid pace,
Comes their youngest daughter, Maggie, with a
    happy, smiling face ;
In her hand she holds a letter from their dear
    ones far away—
" Now listen, father, mother, and I'll tell you
    what they say."

She reads how John is thriving in the busy
    English town,
And how at Christmas he will send his mother a
    silk gown ;
And Mary sends her love, and trusts that mother
    dear keeps strong,
She hopes to get a holiday and see them all ere
    long.

" Will father's bees this year do well ? and how
    is Maggie's cat ?"
'Tis Mary asks, you may be sure, a question such
    as that,
And Mary, too, it is who tells about the church
    so grand,
Where at the prayers the people kneel and at
    the singing stand.

" Where every window," so she writes, " is like
    a picture fair,
The Bible stories told on glass in colours rich
    and rare ;
And all the choir are dressed in white, and they
    so sweetly sing,
Whilst softly a grand organ plays—a horrid
    Popish thing."

" Well, Jim, what sport ?" the father cries, for
    lo ! another one
Hath joined this happy family group ; it is the
    student son,
Set free from college for a time, at liberty to
    roam
Across the hills and through the glens around
    his well-loved home.

" What sport ?" he says, and proudly shows his
    creel of trout so fine,
Tells how a two-pound fish he had, a " beauty "
    on his line,
And yet—he cannot just tell why—it somehow
    got away,
But better luck he hopes to have on a forthcoming
    day.

This happy group again I see as in the days of
    yore,
I in the dear old garden stand among them all
    once more ;
I feel the scent of roses sweet, I hear the mur-
    muring stream,
I raise my hand to pluck a rose—and, lo ! 'tis
    but a dream.

And I am in my attic room, instead of garden
    fair,
With chimney cans instead of flowers around me
    everywhere ;
How strange I should so clearly hear the hum of
    bees again !
Alas! 'tis just a big blue fly upon my window
    pane.

❈

Annie.

OWN the glen on a summer eve
 Came Annie, the village belle,
My darling fair; I waited her there—
 For I loved her, oh! so well.
Her auburn hair made a halo fair
 Around her queenly head,
It gleamed and shone like a golden crown
 In the evening sunlight red.

Long we sat 'neath the old oak tree,
 For, oh! it was hard to part;
I said, "I'll be true, my darling, to yon;
 Good-bye, my bonnie sweetheart."
At break of day I sailed far away
 Over the ocean wide;
When my native shore I could see no more
 I longed to be by her side.

I stood again 'neath the old oak tree,
    When many long years had flown ;
The tree was bare, but I did not care,
    I stood 'neath its boughs alone.
My darling fair, with her auburn hair,
    I'd never meet there again—
For she had been found, they told me, drowned
    In the river in the glen.

Down the glen on a winter day,
    To stand 'neath our old oak tree,
She strayed in a dream—into the stream
    Had slipped whilst thinking of me.
A tress so fair of her auburn hair,
    A ring, and on the hillside
A grassy mound, were all I found
    When I came to claim my bride.

The Dying Student.

IN a dull, dark city chamber, on a rude, hard
    bed there lay
One whose life, so full of promise, now was ebh-
    ing fast away;
Kneeling close beside his pillow was his dearest
    student friend,
Who would snatch from sleep and study precious
    hours with him to spend.

"Dear old chum, dont look so doleful; I am now
    from all pain free,
And my mind is quite clear also. Oh! God has
    been good to me;
He has lent me strength to give you, ere I pass
    from earth away,
Messages to send that loved one who is far from
    me to-day.

" You will tell my darling mother how I never
    once forgot
All her kindly words of counsel and the lessons
    she had taught ;
And though evil was around me, by God's help
    I never fell,
And how I have blessed her teaching you will
    not forget to tell.

" Our professor's little daughter brought me
    some sweet flowers to-day ;
It was Isobel, you know, Jim, her with whom I
    used to play ;
There were lilies and sweet roses, and I found
    among the rest
One small sprig of purple heather, which, of
    course, I liked the best.

" She'd remembered how I love it, for when in
    the park we'd roam
I would talk to her of mother and describe my
    Highland home ;
How she kissed and clung about me, and, poor
    child, how she did cry
When to-day I gently told her she must now bid
    me good-bye.

"And to-morrow when they tell her I am dead
    she'll weep, I know,
But through time she will forget me, and, of
    course, 'tis better so;
She is but a child, you know, Jim, and a child's
    life should be bright— ,
Sorrow, grief, and bitter trials all too soon will
    mar the light.

"There's another—she's the sister of my little
    Isobel—
Will she weep or think about me when she hears
    my fun'ral knell?
She is beautiful, you know, Jim, and as good as
    she is fair,
Hazel eyes so grave and wistful, and so soft and
    dark her hair.

"Oh! her voice was kind and gentle, and her
    smile so bright and sweet,
And she always spoke so kindly when we some-
    times chanced to meet;
With dear Isobel I'd wander by the hour, while
    she would tell
Of her dark-eyed, well-loved sister. Did she
    guess I loved as well?

"Yes, I broke my heart about her, and my love
     she never guessed ;
Why should she, so wealthy, lovely, fit to mate
     with Scotland's best ?
I was just a poor young student, brilliant but of
     low degree,
And a favourite with her father ; so she, too, was
     kind to me.

"Now, old chum, you know my secret, of my
     love I'm not ashamed ;
Though I now am dying for her, she must not
     at all be blamed ;
I could never hope to win her, and I could not
     live to see
What would have made life so lovely given to
     some one else than me.

"Let my grave be near the footpath leading to
     the house of prayer—
She will pass by every Sabbath as she goes to
     worship there ;
When the grass is green above it bring my little
     friend to see,
She will show it to her sister, and, perhaps,
     she'll think of me.

" Good-bye, now, for I am weary, and I long to
    be at rest,
Ere I sleep, please read a chapter from the Book
    we love the best ;
I will wait for you, for mother, for *her* on the
    other side,
She will know there how I loved her ; good-bye,
    Jim !" and so he died.

In the Workhouse.

"What God hath joined together let not man put asunder."

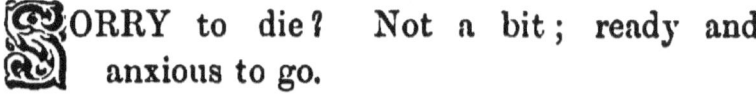

SORRY to die? Not a bit; ready and anxious to go.
I longed to die two years ago, had the Lord willed it so,
For I'm no use now on earth—only a " cumb'rer " they say ;
And, oh ! it is hard for me to live thus on charity.

Why was I brought so low? Well, 'twas through no fault of my own—
Many, alas ! must reap the seeds that others have sown.
Jean and I were alone, all those who had known us were dead ;
What a hard struggle I had to earn our daily bread,

When I grew too old for work starvation stared
    in our face,
No one to help us seemed near, no one to pity
    our case ;
My heart had to echo Jean's words, though it
    grew heavy as lead,
As "John, we must go to the House," my poor
    old wife to me said.

Oh ! it was hard to leave the cottage, where long
    years ago
I brought my bonnie young wife, when the hills
    were covered with snow—
The cottage where Nan and Jean and little
    Jamie were born,
The home where they withered away, leaving
    us so forlorn.

Would we had died when they died, for now, in
    the evening of life,
A greater trouble than death had fallen on me
    and the wife—
Dead to each other we were, for in the House we
    must part ;
Ere Jean had been in two months she died of a
    broken heart.

I was made of tougher stuff, so I am still here,
    you see,
But soon I am going now, with Jean and the
    bairns to be.
Sorry to die? Not a bit; so ready to go, my
    dear,
I long to go forth from this House, so big, and
    cold, and drear.

Oh! happy husbands and wives, you who with
    riches are blest,
Think of those here in the House when by your
    firesides you rest,
Happy with those you love, knowing nothing but
    death can part
Those joined together in love, one in mind, in
    spirit, and heart.

"Those whom the Lord hath joined let nothing
    asunder break,"
This means both the rich and poor; oh! will
    you help us for His sake?
Though I need naught now for self, I plead for
    hundreds to-night—
Will no one stretch forth a hand to make so
    many lives bright?

In the Twilight.

GOING home in the twilight,
  Under the leafy trees ;
Going home in the twilight,
  Fanned by the summer breeze ;
Going home in the twilight,
  Feeling so glad and gay ;
Going home in the twilight,
  At close of a summer day.

Going home in the twilight,
  Over the moorland wide ;
Going home in the twilight,
  With someone by my side.
Going home in the twilight
  With someone's hand in mine,
And someone's eyes upon me,
  From whose grey depths love doth shine.

Going home in the twilight,
  Listening to words so sweet,
While someone bending o'er me
  Doth the old, old tale repeat;
Going home in the twilight,
  While stars peep out above,
And flowers and breeze and river
  Seem all to sing of love.

Going home in the twilight
  With one who loves me well;
Going home in the twilight
  With joy unspeakable;
Going home in the twilight
  With him whom all through life
I've promised to walk with ever,
  As his companion and wife.

Two Pictures of Home.

WHAT IT WAS.

A CHEERLESS room, a living tomb,
  So damp, unhealthy, cold ;
A cupboard bare, a broken chair,
  A mattress torn and old.

A woman thin, some food to win,
  Is stitching through the night,
The cold her nips, two farthing dips
  Are all her heat and light.

Curses and blows are all she knows
  Of husband's love or care ;
She toils for him till eyes are dim,
  While he does drink and swear.

A baby lies, and piteous cries
  Upon the mattress old,
Its cries for bread are wild and dread,
  Its limbs are stiff with cold.

1

The baby dies before her eyes,
    Her heart is like to break ;
Her light is done, work scarce begun—
    She sobs, "Me also take."

A drunkard's wife !   Oh ! what a life
    Of misery and woe ;
A drunkard's child ! scorned and reviled
    Wherever she may go.

Oft death they greet with welcome sweet,
    From hunger, cold, and pain,
He brings relief ; forgot's their grief
    When God's bright home they gain.

WHAT IT MIGHT HAVE BEEN.

A cottage bright, so warm and light,
    A garden trim and gay ;
A little child, so merry, wild,
    Among the flowers at play.

A woman neat, with smile so sweet,
    The supper doth prepare ;
Comfort is found in all around,
    She knows no want nor care.

A merry shout she hears without
From Jean, their lassie wild,
Her husband dear she knows is near,
She hears him greet his child.

With kisses sweet his wife doth greet
This husband, true and kind.
More homes like this, where all is bliss,
Oh ! how we long to find.

A Call to Service.

THE sky was blue and cloudless as a fair
    Italian sky,
On such a day 'twas perfect joy beneath the
    trees to lie ;
How pleasant 'twas to listen to the brook as it
    did pass,
To watch the flickering foliage casting shadows
    on the grass.

As I lay 'twixt sleep and waking on that lovely
    summer day,
The merry stream, the waving grass, both
    seemed to fade away ;
'Neath the trees I was not lying, but I stood on
    a fair shore,
And I looked around in wonder, for I'd ne'er
    been there before.

I gazed in speechless rapture on a scene so pass-
 ing fair,
The loveliest spot I'd seen on earth could not
 with this compare ;
And a great joy thrilled my being, for I knew
 that I did stand
By that river, clear as crystal, in the lovely
 Better Land.

'Midst the white-robed throng around me, the
 redeemed of every race,
There was one with eyes so loving, and with
 kind and gentle face ;
And the angels harping round him " Hosannah ?"
 loud did sing,
And I knelt in lowly reverence in the presence
 of my King.

He smiled so kindly on me, and He laid upon
 my head
Those dear hands by sharp nails piercéd, and He
 gently to me said—
" My commands, oh ! brave young soldier, will
 you go forth to fulfil ?"
Quick, with tears of joy, I murmured—" Yes,
 dear Lord, I will, I will."

"There's a corner of My vineyard I now will
    send you to,
You will find in that vast city a great work for
    Me to do ;
Trust Me in your hours of darkness, and, when
    battling 'gainst sin's tide,
Be not fearful, but remember I am ever on your
    side.

"I do not bid you serve Me far away on foreign
    shore,
For how many do not know Me dwelling near
    your very door ?
Exhort, and warn, and teach them till each one
    in Me believes ;
Now, go forth, oh ! youthful reaper, and return
    with many sheaves."

I awoke beneath the starlight, for the sun had
    long since set,
Woke with heart so full of gladness, though my
    cheeks with tears were wet ;
I knelt beside the brooklet and poured forth my
    soul in prayer,
And my life and work from henceforth I gave to
    my Master there. . . .

My poor life with all its blunders, which daily do
    me grieve,
He, the pure and perfect Saviour, has been will-
    ing to receive ;
He has been well pleased the increase to give to
    seed I've sown,
He has given me many jewels to present before
    His throne.

Our Parson.

"One act of charity will teach us more of the love of God
than a thousand sermons."—F. W. ROBERTSON.

"CLUMSY? Well, maybe you're right,
　　His manner to you may seem rough;
But listen, and then you'll admit
　　Our parson's made of good stuff.

"You see yon hovel down there?
　　At the time when small-pox was bad,
A miner, the owner of it,
　　The loathsome, dread disease had.

"He had not a friend in the world
　　To care whether he lived or died,
Except our parson, who watched
　　Night and day by the man's bedside.

"He was known as 'Big, Swearing Bill,'
　　And in all the countryside round
A coarser, worse man than he
　　None, I am sure, could have found.

" When our parson came to this place,
   'Mongst the rest, he went to see Bill ;
When he talked of religion Bill swore,
   And threatened the parson to kill.

" Then Bill did all that he' could
   The gentleman kind to annoy,
But his influence good in the place
   Bill strove in vain to destroy.

" Yet still there were many ways
   In which he could vex Mr Blank ;
For many an unhappy hour
   Our parson had Big Bill to thank.

" Things went on like this for some months,
   Until, as I told you before,
Bill took the small-pox, and lay
   For days and weeks at death's door.

" He had not a friend in the world—
   He'd shown himself friendly to none ;
And being a bear all his life,
   Was detested by every one,

" Except our parson so good,
  Who'd most cause of all to detest,
But who watched by that sick bed instead—
  I suppose you can guess the rest ?

" Bill rose from that bed a changed man,
  Many lessons he'd learned there ;
The deed our parson had done
  Taught him more than preaching or prayer.

" ' Clumsy ' you thought him and ' rough ?'
  ' Not suited a town charge to fill ?'
Perhaps not, though he's *perfect* to me,
  And no wonder—for I am Bill."

The Child of Hale.

A LANCASHIRE LEGEND.

E stood within the churchyard old, one
    fair, sweet April day,
Beside a rough-hewn, moss-grown stone, 'neath
    which a giant lay—
" Here lies one who was 9 ft. 3," I read, " the
    child of Hale ;"
Then to my friend I said, " Can you tell me this
    giant's tale !"

She said—" The story goes that once upon a
    summer day,
A boy down by the Mersey's side upon the beach
    did stray ;
There, in a fit of frolic wild, upon the sand he
    made
A mark o'er nine feet long—that he might grow
    that length he prayed.

" Then carelessly he cast himself down on the
    mark he drew,
And while he slept there on the beach he slowly
    longer grew,
Till ere the sun that summer night had sunk
    into the sea,
The boy awoke to find that he had grown to nine
    feet three.

" What trade was his, or how he lived, has,
    'midst the mists of time,
Been lost; we only know he lived some years
    beyond his prime,
Only this stone of ponderous length is left to tell
    the tale
Of the giant who, in irony, was called the
    ' Child of Hale.' "

Flora.

A BALLAD.

"YOU ask me for my daughter's hand,"
   The haughty chieftain cried ;
" You say you love each other well ?
   You want her for your bride ?
You say this union would blot out
   The feud that's lasted long
Between our clans !—know, foolish youth,
   Forbes ne'er forgives a wrong.
No, by my faith ! you never shall
   My lovely Flora wed ;
I'd rather give her to a serf—
  . I'd rather see her dead.
Take then your answer and begone,
   And, foolish youth, beware !
If near my home you're found again,
   You'll die, a prisoner, there."

Proudly young Campbell turned away
　And ne'er a word did speak,
Although a frown was on his brow,
　And hotly burned his cheek ;
"Revenge is sweet," he thought, "and I
　Will have it, haughty chief,
So guard your treasure carefully,
　For cunning is the thief."

The sound of merry jest and song
　Went ringing through the hall,
For this was Flora's birthday night,
　And she was queen of all ;
Yet sad she sat, nor cared to join
　In song or dance or jest,
Because her father proud had spurned
　The one she loved the best.

Into the hall, with falt'ring step,
　An agèd minstrel came,
And no one knew from whence he was,
　And no one knew his name ;
He sang of love and loyal hearts,
　His voice was wondrous sweet ;
The jesters ceased their jests, to hear, ·
　The dancers stayed their feet.

"Come, sit you here," the chieftain cried,
  "And sup, oh ! reverend sire,
For surely workman such as you
  Is worthy of his hire ;
And you shall have a bag of gold,
  For never did I hear
A lovelier song than you have sung,
  A voice more sweet and clear."

"I thank you for your words so kind,"
  The agèd minstrel said,
"And for the gold you've promised me,
  The feast for me you've spread ;
But for these things I do not care,
  And I would rather crave
Your lovely daughter for one dance,
  Oh ! chieftain, true and brave."

Then, midst the mazes of the dance,
  He whispered in her ear—
"Meet me beside the wicket gate,
  I've news for you, my dear."

They've met beside the wicket gate—
  The minstrel old and grey
She sees no more ; before her stands
  Her lover young and gay.
A kiss—a hasty word—and ere
  From her proud father's hall
She has been missed, she's o'er the hills
  With him loved best of all.

The Drunkard's Wife.

"OH! Willie, stay with me to-night,
    The last night of the year;
Twelve months to-night since we were wed—
    Stay with me, Willie dear.

" Our baby's ill, and I am lone
    When you are at the Rink ;
Oh, Willie, do not go to-night—
    Give up the cursed drink.

" Our cottage wee was clean and neat,
    The brightest in the row ;
But things have one by one been sold—
    For drink they've had to go.

" Our garden once was bright and gay,
    Well stocked with flowers fair ;
But now they're withered all away,
    For them you've ceased to care.
        J

"Oh ! Willie, do not go to-night,
  It is so lonely here ;
Together let us happy be,
  As happy as last year."

" I must go, or the lads will think
  I'm ill, if here I stay ;
I'll only take a glass of beer,
  And then I'll come away."

He closed the door—the mother sat
  And hushed the wailing child ;
She listened for her husband's step,
  And prayed in accents wild.

The hours passed on, the fire was out,
  The cottage dark and chill ;
An angel bright passed through the room,
  And whispered, " Peace, be still."

His cheerless home the drunkard reached
  When midnight was at hand,
Entered, with reeling step, this slave
  To the curse of Britain's land.

The morning dawned, the drunkard woke
   From his sound, drunken sleep;
As glad bells chimed the new-born year,
   He woke, alas! to weep.

So still, sat by the empty grate
   The wife he'd sore oppressed;
Her arms still clasped her dear, dead babe
   Close to her frozen breast.

He called her name, she answered not—
   She could not hear his cries;
Her grief was o'er, the babe and she
   Were safe in Paradise.

Longing.

LONG to feel the breezes from my native
    mountains blow,
I long to stand beside the stream where
    Tummel's waters flow,
I long to see my dear old house in Gernaig's
    peaceful glen ;
Oh ! could I but be there to-day, I'd soon be
    strong again.

I care not for my palace home, nor for my
    boundless wealth,
For I have lost what's worth far more—that
    priceless treasure, health ;
I languish in this country fair, beneath the
    bright blue skies ;
Oh ! give me back my native land, where rugged
    mountains rise.

I care not for the balmy air, which comes so
    soft and mild ;
Oh ! let me feel the mountain breeze, which
    blows so fresh and wild ;
The odour of the orange groves is not so sweet
    to me
As that of homely purple heath, which blooms
    so fair and free.

Oh ! give me back my dear old home, e'en
    humble though it be,
Its memories now are very sweet, 'tis "all the
    world" to me ;
'Twas there I played, a happy child, and then a
    careless boy—
'Twas there I lived, a' father's pride, a mother's
    hope and joy.

'Twas there one night, now long ago, I bade
    these two good-bye ;
Ah ! how I longed the world to see, to make a
    fortune try—
And now I'm very rich, but of what use is wealth
    to me ?
In comfort would we three have lived—now
    home I'll never see.

I'll send my parents dear my gold, 'twill useful
    be I know,
Although they'd rather have their boy, it must
    be better so ;
And Paradise, that better land, will fairer seem
    to me
Than that dear rugged mountain land where
    now I long to be.

Our Bill.

"NO, don't go that way ;, let us go round,
  Under the bridge then over the mound."

"Why, man alive, are you going that way ?
This is the nearer by far, I should say."

"Yes, mate, but you could not there cross the
  line,
Did it bring to your mind what it does to mine.

"You're a stranger here, so you do not know
What happened our little Bill years ago.

"He was the dearest child ever I knew,
And in my long life I've known not a few.

"A regular pickle, not one moment still,
Yet always so winning was little Bill.

"Well, I sometimes think that the wife and me
Loved him too much, and were punished, you
  see ;

"' Keep your eye on Bill,' did I often say,
' And don't let him go near the line to play.

" Then I'd lift him up and try to explain
The danger that lay in a passing train.

" But he'd laugh at me and shake his small
    head—
' Dad wont let his engine hurt Bill,' he aye said.

" One summer night the express was late ;
I wondered if Bill at the curve would wait—

" For the signal I gave him aye as we passed.
We dashed round the curve, and I stood
    aghast—

" Fifty yards in front, his head on the line,
There, sound asleep, lay this darling of mine !

" My tongue was frozen, I could not scream ;
I stood like one wakened out of a dream.

" 'Twas too late to stop her ; my heart stood
    still—
A jolt—' Dad's engine ' had killed little Bill !

" So that is the reason I cannot bear
To cross the line near the curve just there."

My Little Ben.

LOVED him? You don't know how well,
    for somehow I never can speak
Of Ben, for a lump in my throat, and the tears
    running down my cheek.
I'll tell you about him, Miss, though I never
    could speak to the men
Of my child; they'd laugh at my tears—you see
    they didn't know Ben.

Oh! shall I ever forget that cold, stormy, dark,
    winter morn,
When at breakfast time I came home to find a
    son had been born,
And my life-long sweetheart, my wife for one
    year only, was dead,
Whilst I was left all alone with a helpless infant
    instead.

Well, Miss, my little Ben thrived, though how I
　　scarcely can tell,
For his mother he must have missed, though,
　　for the sake of my Nell,
I did what I could for the child, and he grew
　　fairer each day—
So like, oh! so very like, my loved darling far,
　　far away.

At nights, when together at home, how Ben
　　would prattle to me
(He was so interesting now, a fair-haired laddie
　　of three)
Of wheels and engines and trains, for about those
　　things he seemed mad;
Though my days were spent 'mong such things,
　　to hear him talk thus made me sad.

Why I felt sad I don't know, though sometimes
　　a warning of ill
Would come and o'ershadow my life, my heart
　　with anxious thoughts fill;
But I smiled at my childish fears, for Ben was
　　so safe with me—
At least *I* thought so, but the Lord thought
　　otherwise, Miss, you see.

I was pointsman down at the junction, fifteen
    miles south from here,
Half-a-mile from my lonely cottage—I'd been
    there many a year ;
I'd no one to leave with Ben when I went to
    work each day,
So I always took him with me, and all day long
    he would play

On the floor of my pointsman's box, were the day
    stormy or wet,
Or if it were fine he'd climb on the banks fair
    flowers to get ;
He'd laugh and frolic and sing along by the side
    of the line,
Whilst I, with a loving care, would watch o'er
    this darling of mine.

The winter my laddie was five, I took a pain in
    my head,
I could get no sleep at nights, 'twas "rheumatics,"
    the doctor said ;
Ah ! then how I longed for my wife, for 'tis when
    a man's unwell
That he misses a woman's kind care, and sadly I
    missed my Nell.

I sat by the fire in my box one cold, frosty,
    winter day,
With Ben on the floor at my feet, so happy
    engaged in play ;
The child's voice seemed to grow faint, I could
    scarcely hear what he said,
The newspaper dropped from my hand several
    times as I read.

I must have fallen asleep—I started up with a
    cry,
I was alone—where was Ben ?   Oh ! God, had the
    south train passed by ?
Ah ! no, I would just be in time to clear the line
    for the mail,
And draw the lever to shunt the south train to
    the other rail.

I ran with the speed of the wind, for I saw the
    mail from the north,
Not half-a-mile ahead, with a scream from the
    tunnel come forth ;
At the same moment I heard the train from the
    south coming down,
Bowling along at the rate of a mile a minute to
    town.

Where was Ben? My heart stood still as I
gazed down the iron way—
There, with his head on the rail, fast asleep, my
little child lay.
To draw the lever and shunt the south train
meant death to my boy—
Not to draw it would save my child, but how
many lives destroy?

"One life or one hundred, oh! God, must I give
back now to thee?
The one, my darling, my all; the hundred so
little to me—
So little to me, yet each the dearest to some
other one,
Children as dear to their fathers as e'er was my
darling son."

These thoughts, which take so long to tell, passed
through my mind like a flash;
In a moment the trains would have met—I
seemed to hear the dread crash;
But the path of duty was plain; the lever I
drew—bent my head;
When I raised it the trains had rushed past; I
stood alone with my dead.

Yes, Miss, here this summer night a murderer
    before you I stand,
With the blood of my only child, my darling, red
    on my hand ;
But I feel the Lord has forgiven, and I'll be
    happy again
When I get up yonder, and meet my wife and
    dear little Ben.

Millie.

THE little face was stained with tears,
    The naked shoulders pinched and blue;
She crouched upon a cold door step,
    And her thin shawl tight round her drew.

I saw her as I hurried past—
    "Oh! Millie, child, why sit you here?
Poor little one, you'll die of cold;
    Come home with me now, Millie, dear."

She raised her tear-dimmed eyes to mine,
    And shook her pretty, curly head—
"No, thanks; dad put me out when drunk,
    But I'll go home when he's in bed."

I watched her father day by day
    Grow more repulsive, sin-defiled;
God thought him not too vile to save—
    His instrument, a little child.

"Millie!" the drunkard said one day,
  As she his breakfast did prepare ;
"Millie, I've been so cruel to you,
  What makes you for your father care ?"

"It's mother, dad ; she comes from Heaven,
  And by my bed each night she stands,
And smiles so sweetly down on me,
  And smooths my hair, and clasps my hands.

"And then, in whispers soft and low,
  She bids me aye for you to care ;
She knows you sometimes take too much,
  But tells me never to despair.

"'Please, Jesus, make dad good again,'
  She comes and whispers in my ear ;
She bids me say that every night,
  For even a child will Jesus hear."

Hot tears coursed down the drunkard's cheeks ;
  He wept then like a little child—
"Oh ! God, be merciful to me,
  So vile a sinner—stained, defiled."

·   ·   ·

In a neat cottage Millie dwells,
  So happy all the livelong day ;
The birds sing in the garden fair,
  The house is decked with roses gay.

And happy as the birds and flowers
  Is Millie, by the window there,
As, when her daily work is done,
  She kneels beside her father's chair.

His hand rests on her curly head,
  He looks at her with eyes of love,
Then kisses that small hand which led
  Him from sin's paths to look above.

"Love's Young Dream."

THE Fairies' Knoll, the Fairies' Knoll,
  There oft, in days gone by,
We sat together hand in hand,
  So happy, Will and I.

The merry stream, the merry stream,
  Rushed noisily along,
While to our youthful ears there seemed
  No music like its song.

The setting sun, the setting sun,
  Shone redly through the trees,
The blackbird's evening hymn of praise
  Was borne upon the breeze.

        .   .   .   .

The Fairies' Knoll, the Fairies' Knoll,
  Have ages long gone by
Since on the mossy knoll we sat,
  So happy, Will and I?

'Tis but five months, 'tis but five months,
  Since the last summer night
We sat together on the knoll,
  Our lives so joyous bright.

The leafy trees, the leafy trees,
  Are leafless now and bare;
The icy breath of Winter's King
  Has fallen everywhere.

The old churchyard, the old churchyard,
  Lies peaceful on the hill;
And in it lies my broken heart,
  Beside my own true Will.

Mistaken.

"LIFT me a little higher; there is something
  I would say,
A word of warning I must speak before I pass
  away;
Come close beside me, dear young friend, my
  voice begins to fail,
But yet I feel I dare not die until I've told my
  tale.

"Thrice ten long years have backward rolled;
  with joy I go once more
(My student days just left behind the best of
  life before)
To tell of Christ and work for Him amid the
  city's hum,
To bear the light of Gospel truth to many a
  darksome slum.

" Why did my zeal so soon grow cold, what filled
    me with unrest ?
Was it the bitter strifes of sects that thus my
    soul oppressed ?
Surely in some lone country charge from these I
    would be free—
The town I left, but still there was no peace of
    mind for me.

" I thought there was a want of life where I had
    come to toil,
The people's hearts I found as dull as their own
    hard clay soil,
In vain I tried them to arouse, to talk to them
    of God ;
Quite sick at heart, I said at length that I must
    go abroad.

" Had I done right ?　Why was that thought for
    ever in my mind ?
Was I, even here in Canada, no perfect peace to
    find ?
I'd broken a fond mother's heart, was that like
    a good son ?
'Twas hard to leave her all alone, yet *Duty* must
    be done.

"Why was my sleep disturbed by dreams so
    horrible and wild,
In which I'd see the piteous face of many an err-
    ing child?
The dwellers in that city's slums would seem to
    me to say—
'Oh! surely there was work at home; why did
    you go away?'

"Had I done right?   Through all these years,
    on to life's very close,
That question ever in my mind, I could find no
    repose.
Had I done right?   On my death-bed the same
    thought tortures so,
For fallen ones I might have raised and
    drunkards answer—"No!"

"Mayhap my work in Canada has not been
    all in vain,
Yet had I but those thirty years to spend for
    Christ again,
I would not flee to foreign lands because of party
    strife;
If not 'Mis-spent,' 'Mistaken,' friend, might
    well be called my life.

"My dear young friend, a warning take from
    what to-night I've said ;
That path in which I've stumbled so, you are
    about to tread ;
Fear not, take for your motto, 'Trust in God
    and do the right,'
And whatso'er you find to do, oh! do it with
    your might.

"To work for Christ you need not go away to
    foreign shore,
The harvest fields are lying white around your
    very door ;
Discouragements, annoyances, you'll find *where'er*
    you go—
What lieth next, oh! do the best, and peace of
    mind you'll know."

An Ivy Spray.

IVY—I CLING TO THEE.

'TWAS close by the church; you know the
place
Where the ivy climbs to the tower high,
Where the turf is always so soft and green,
And the stream goes merrily singing by?
'Twas there one evening to me was told
That wonderful tale, ever new yet so old.

He plucked a spray of the ivy green,
As we stood together 'neath sunset skies,
And, bending low, he gave it to me,
With a merry light in his dark brown eyes—
"Do you know its meaning, my friend," he said;
I answered nothing, but shook my head.

His eyes were reading my very soul,
Mine fell before their keen, earnest gaze ;
My heart beat so loud that he must have heard,
And my cheeks would most provokingly blaze.
He smiled, as if something pleasant he read,
And something very like " darling " he said.

Then, somehow, I found his arm round my
    waist,
And his dark, handsome head bent down close to
    mine ;
While his soft brown eyes, which I'd always
    admired,
Seemed now with a beautiful light to shine ;
And Love was no more an empty sound,
And Life for me a new charm had found.

Soon we were parted ; I'd long to wait—
What did that matter when he was true !
Whenever impatient I'd wander away
Up to the church where the ivy grew ;
There his soft words would come back to me—
" Sweetheart, remember ' I cling to thee !' "

True to his promise, he came at last,
Bringing a sweet orange blossom spray ;
Fondly he kissed me, and whispered low—
" Dear little Faithful, now name the day."
He's minister now where the ivy does grow,
And I'm his right hand—at least, he says so.

My Queen

OWN the path, through the flowery glade—
  Oh ! she was fair, so fair to see—
Tripping along, came a gentle maid—
  Oh ! she was dear, so dear to me ;
Eyes as blue as the summer sky,
  Hair of a wondrous golden sheen ;
Modest was she, retiring and shy,
  But so bewitching, my queen, my queen.

Under the leafy boughs we strayed,
  Hand in hand, through the summer days,
While the squirrels around us played,
  While the birds sang their hymns of praise ;
Bluer the blue sky than ever before,
  Brighter the days than they ever had been,
Everything round us a smiling face wore—
  Because of her presence, my queen, my queen,

Ah ! our bliss was too great to last,
　　Clouds came over our azure sky—
Nipped was she by the wintry blast ;
　　Broken-hearted, I watched her die.
Through the glade we shall walk no more,
　　But, away in that land unseen,
Tears and partings for ever o'er,
　　She is waiting, my queen, my queen.

Found Dead.

THE trade got much worse every week, sir,
   Firm after firm went down ;
And we were on short time ourselves soon—
  Ours, the largest business in town.

Our master paid off his men next,
   It grieved him, but what could he do ?
There wasn't work for the 'prentice lads,
  So, of course, I was paid off, too.

That night, as I sat in our cottage,
   With my bairns and dear little wife,
With tears I said—" Wife, I am idle ;"
  Ah ! that night how dark seemed my life.

She cheered me, although her lips quivered,
   As she looked at baby and Vi ;
Then gently said—" Perhaps you'll get work
    soon ;
  I know my dear husband will try.

Try ! Day after day, sir, I wandered
　　Through the town in sunshine or rain,
Asking, pleading for something to do,
　　But asking and pleading in vain.

We'd pawned everything we could want, sir ;
　　Our dear little home looked so bare
Without the clock and the cradle,
　　The pictures, my wife's rocking chair.

Times grew worse, and life was so dark, sir ;
　　God cares for His creatures, I've read,
But, oh, it was hard to believe it,
　　With our children crying for bread.

Our baby, our golden-haired darling,
　　Was dying for want, sir, of food ;
And my wife and Vi were so wasted,
　　I couldn't say, " God's ways are good."

One night I had wandered away, sir,
　　Out under the cold winter sky—
I couldn't stay in any longer,
　　Watching our little one die.

I saw at a grocer's door hanging
    A very small sack of oatmeal ;
I eagerly longed to possess it,
    But conscience said, " Thou shalt not steal."

But conscience and right were forgotten,
    In a moment the meal I did take ;
I never would have stolen for self, sir,
    'Twas for my dear baby's sake.

" Stop, thief," came the cry in a moment,
    At once I was marched off to jail ;
There those shelpit faces did haunt me,
    And I heard my little one's wail.

Released in a week, I rushed homewards,
    To find our home empty and bare,
And my wife and bairns, said the neighbours,
    Gone away they didn't know where.

Found dead !—did I hear some one saying ?
    Found dead on the cold, stony street,
A woman and two little children—
    " Found dead !" did I wildly repeat.

Sir, 'tis years since my awful bereavement,
    But, when the poor ask me for bread,
I give them both food and shelter,
    For the sake of the dear ones found dead.

A Street Incident.

NARROW, dismal street,
　　One of our city's slums,
Where the air is never fresh and sweet,
　　And the sunlight never comes—
There the pale-faced children play
In the gutter all the day.

A rush of horses' feet,
　　A cry from women who stand
Gossiping here and there on the street,
　　An idle, tawdry band—
"Losh me ! the wee lassie Broun
By the horse has been knockit doun."

Bruised is the little form,
　　There's blood on the golden hair,
And the sweet baby face is ghastly white—
　　For Death is written there.
One moment happy and gay ;
The next, a morsel of clay.

L

Where's her mother—who knows ?
  Break gently the awful news ;
What need ?   She is seldom sober, with blows
  The child she did ever abuse ;
Her death the mother won't heed,
'Twill be one less to clothe and feed.

Where is her father, then ?
  Leading a convict's life,
Sent away from his fellow men
  For trying to murder his wife.
Jesus His lamb has set free
From a life of misery.

'Tis but a Little Faded Flower.

'TIS but a little faded flower; sweet
   thoughts it brings to me
Of one glad hour spent long ago beside the
   summer sea,
When in the golden evening light we wandered
   hand-in-hand,
Out from the busy, noisy town, across the yellow
   sand.

Your soft dark eyes were bent on me, and in their
   depths I read
That wond'rous tale, not new, not old, whilst
   smilingly you said,
(As out among the rough sea grass you plucked
   this little flower,)
" Take this, and keep it, Flora, dear, in memory
   of this hour."

I took the hardy, wild sea pink, I have it safely
    still,
Though it has faded long ago, I keep it ever will;
But, ah ! I do not need the flower to bring again
    to me
Sweet memories of that happy hour beside the
    summer sea.

Tho' in a Lowland town you now are from me far
    away,
Yet to my Highland home I know you will come
    back some day ;
And in the evening light we'll walk, while you'll
    repeat to me
That wond'rous tale you told that night beside
    the summer sea.

He Cometh Not.

SHE was standing by the window,
　　A maiden sweet and fair,
With bright eyes of dazzling azure,
　　And soft curling golden hair;
But her rosy lips were pouting
　　As she watched the garden gate,
And her pretty face was clouded
　　As she thought, "He is so late."

They had parted plighted lovers
　　Last night by the ballroom door;
She, now standing by the window,
　　The scene again lived o'er.
His glance, his clinging hand-clasp,
　　His whisper in her ear—
"Good-bye till to-morrow, Elsie,
　　Then I'll see your father, dear."

She was watching for his coming
  O'er the moor so dazzling white,
Trying hard to pierce the darkness
  Of the quickly gathering night;
Till a voice broke through the stillness,
  " Elsie, child, why stand you there ?
Light the lamp and draw the curtains ;
  Come and sit by daddy's chair."

All night the snow whirled madly,
  Wrapping earth in a white shroud ;
And across the waste of moorland
  The wild North wind shrieked loud ;
And the angry waves dashed hoarsely
  On the distant rocky coast ;
And a trusting maid watched vainly
  For the one she loved the most.

Many noble ships had foundered
  Ere that awful night had sped,
And many a heart was desolate,
  And many a tear was shed ;
And a bright, young life was darkened,
  Which had been so glad before ;
And a hopeless maid watched vainly
  For the one who'd come no more.

On the lonely moor they found him
  Asleep at dawn of day—
The icicles were in his hair,
  The snow upon him lay;
In his hand were clasped the roses
  Which his fair-haired darling wore—
The roses she had given him
  At the ball the night before.

Collie Jim.

DULL? Yes, mate, it is dull to lie alone
    here all the day;
But all my pain has gone—a sign that death is
    near they say;
And death would welcome be to me, if I were
    only sure
That I would die just like a dog, with nought
    more to endure.

Let women and the young believe in God and
    future state—
Such notions comfort persons weak, I've oft said
    to you, mate;
But I would gladly give these years I've spent
    in sin so wild
If I had now to comfort me the faith of a young
    child.

The parson's lady came and sat beside me here
    to-day ;
She looked so good and kind I could not bid her
    go away ;
She read some Bible words to me, though them
    I don't believe—
Yet, mate, I did not tell her so, for her I could
    not grieve.

And since she went away I've thought that,
    somehow, after all,
There must be something in the thing that folks
    " religion " call,
Else how would she—that lady fair—to such as
    I have read,
Talked sweetly, and her cool hand laid upon my
    aching head ?

That cool hand, somehow, made my eyes with
    burning tears grow dim—
You well may smile ; just fancy, tears in eyes of
    Collier Jim !
It made me think I was a child beside my
    mother's knee,
Her hand upon my curls as from the Book she
    read to me.

I had a godly mother, mate ; to me the greater
    shame
That I've blasphemed and cursed what she
    revered—God's holy name ;
Had I remembered what she read, how different
    far for me
When I go forth to meet her God, if such an one
    there be.

'Tis strange that what the lady said has haunted
    me all day ;
She told me Jesus Christ's own blood would
    wash my sins away,
And that He'd died that I might live in Heaven
    above—you know
That mother often said the same so many years
    ago.

Can it be true ?   Oh ! tell me mate !   Go, fetch
    the Book and read,
You cannot comfort me ?   Ah ! no, I taught you
    my dark creed ;
It cannot light death's unknown path—forget
    it ; and, oh ! mate,
Go, bring the parson's wife to me, before it be
    too late.   .   .   .   .

She entered, and, with hushed footsteps, approached the collier's bed,
Then turnèd to his mate, with tear-dimmed eyes
—for, lo ! the man was dead ;
Without the one true guiding light, into the dark Unknown
Had gone that rudderless, frail bark—all unprepared, alone.

Misunderstood.

 CANNOT leave him all alone, for that night
mother died
She said " Good-bye " to father dear, then called
me to her side,
And made me promise I would be his comfort all
his life—
I cannot leave my father, then, e'en to be
Harold's wife.

I know my father could not live amidst the city's
din,
Though Harold would be proud and glad bread
for us both to win ;
To dwell in some dark, stifling street I know
would father kill—
He could not live without the breeze from his
dear native hill.

'Twas but last night that Harold came and
    talked of love awhile;
I told him it could never be, then tried on him
    to smile—
But, oh! 'twas hard when, angrily, he said I did
    not care,
And that, if I refused him now, 'twould drive
    him to despair.

He'd ne'er have said I did not care (how dark
    life is to-day),
Had he but known, and what it cost to send
    him thus away;
I dare not at the future look, nor think what
    life will be
Without this friend who long has been all the
    wide world to me.

I'll be my father's comfort still, for duty's path
    is plain;
I'll smile upon him as of old—he'll never know
    my pain.
Though Harold thinks me false, and that for him
    I did not care,
There's One above who understands, and He my
    grief will share.

Stranger than Fiction.

SHE was only a poor man's child
    That was why,
When the message was sent,
He never went ;
For the doctor thought—
" 'Twill be one less to feed,
And they won't much heed
Though the child should die."

He was dining from home next day,
    That was why,
When again they sent,
He never went ;
For the doctor enjoyed
His meal, and thought, as he smiled—
" For a poor man's child
Must my pleasure be destroyed ?"

'Twas at length, with a clouded brain,
 To obey
Their wild entreaties he went
When they oft had sent;
But just what was wrong
He could not then say,
But would call next day—
And left, humming a song.

Day dawned, but he did not come;
 And why not?
Then it slowly passed,
Night came at last;
And the watchers did pray
For the Lord to come
And take the child home
Ere another day.

He came sauntering in next night
 With a smile,
Which died as the father said—
" The child is dead !
She might have been saved
Had you come when we sent."
Low the doctor's head bent,
As he pardon craved.

" Let this be a lesson for life,"
     The father said ;
" God grant you ne'er may know
Such depth of woe
As is ours to-night ;
She was dear to the wife and me,
And, though poor folks we be,
We have hearts, and know what is right.

A Prodigal.

"AFT hae grieved ye sairly, say not ye've
    naething to forgie—
What made yer rosy cheeks grow pale, an'
    dimmed yer bricht blue e'e?
For, wife, ye were the bonniest lass in a' the
    country side,
Whan, ten year past, I brocht ye here, my win-
    some, new-made bride.

" Yer cheeks micht hae been rosy still, an' bricht
    yer blue e'en too,
Had I wi' kindness treated ye, as a husband
    aucht to do ;
But ye'll forgie me, Mary, e'er I gang to my
    lang hame,
An' ye'll think upon me kindly whan oor bairnie
    speaks my name.

M

"Ye'll keep the vile drink frae him, for its it
    that's ruined me ;
I vowed whan we were married I a sober man
    wad be—
For ye kent that was my failin', an', agin' yer
    parent's will,
Ye trusted me, my bonnie lass, an', eh ! I saired
    ye ill.

"I tried to keep my promise, but I didna keep
    it lang—
I hadna asked the Lord for strength, an' sae I
    sune gaed wrang ;
An', when aince again I'd tasted, the very Deil
    himsel'
Seemed to catch me in his clutches, an' drag me
    down to hell.

"I'll ne'er forget that e'enin' that I brak the
    pledge I'd taen ;
To oor maister's waddin' supper I had wi' the
    ithers gane,
I had got a bit o' schoolin', so was asked some
    words to say
To toast the bride an' bridegroom, but I quietly
    answered, " Nay."

"What! not toast oor weel-loved maister!" an' a
    hundred pair o' eyes
Were turned upon me as I sat in wonder an'
    surprise ;
Feared for their taunts, I rose wi' haste, sayin',
    'Toast him, mates, I will ;'
Then seized the drink, wi' tremblin' hand, an'
    quick my gless did fill.

"Frae then I was a lost man ; ye ken weel sin'
    that nicht
I hae aye been strayin' far'er frae the narrow
    path o' richt ;
I wonder if the maister, whan he turned me frae
    the mill,
Ever thocht it was his hand to me the first push
    gae doon hill ?

"Ye'll keep the drink frae Davie, an' ye'll tell
    him, wife, some day
Hoo it brings into the blithest hames the direst
    dule an' wae ;
An' ye'll gar him jine teetotal, but ye'll never lat
    him ken
That his faither was a drunkard, despised by his
    fellow-men.

" Oh ! I wish thae years I've wasted were gien
    again to me,
Hoo different I wad spend them noo—I wad be
    kind to ye ;
Ye say that ye've forgien' me, an' ye tell me o'
    Ane wha,
If I'll but lippen to Him, will tak' a' my sins
    awa'.

" Only lippen—that seems easy ; still, d'ye think
    He wad forgie
If He only kent my vileness, an' hoo bad I've
    been to ye ?
Kens it a', an' yet He loes me ?   Oh ! dear wife,
    can that be true ?
Read His lovin' words aince mair, lass, an' I'll
    lippen to Him noo.

" Guid-nicht, noo, for I am weary, an' the day is
    nearly dune,
I shall fa' asleep at e'enin' wi' yon glorious
    settin' sun ;
Kiss me, wife ; forget, forgie, lass,"—then he
    looked at her and smiled ;
And the Father met with gladness his repentant,
    long-lost child.

God's Acre.

FAR from the busy town,
　　With its ceaseless bustle and din,
And hurrying crowds, with restless look,
　　Eager their bread to win—
It lies so peaceful and still
On the slope of a grassy hill.

Far from the cold, hard world,
　　With its ceaseless race for gold,
Its strife and sorrow, and suff'ring and sin,
　　Its hunger and biting cold—
God's acre peacefully lies
Under the sunset skies.

The great red harvest moon
　　Has risen o'er yon green hill,
Flooding the loch with a golden light,
　　And the streamlet by the mill;
'Tis looking so calmly down
On that churchyard far from town.

It shines on a pure white stone
  Where I kneel and gently weep,
For under it those that were my all,
  My darlings, lie asleep—
My husband and bairnies three;
Oh! the world is dark to me.

I miss my husband good,
  For he ever was kind to me;
My heart is aching and bleeding to-day
  For my dear wee bairnies three;
But they're safe from grief and pain,
And I know we shall meet again.

After a few short years,
  With the battle fought and won,
And tears and partings for ever o'er,
  And the perfect life begun—
For evermore I shall be
With my husband and darlings three.

The Way of Salvation.

SHE lay upon a heap of straw in a dark attic
    room,
An agéd woman, who for years had worked a
    small hand loom;
A minister beside her sat, and words of comfort
    read,
Whilst restlessly the suff'rer tossed upon her
    rude, hard bed.

"Oh! sir, he'll no' forgie me noo, for I've been
    oh! sae wild;
For years I've trod destruction's path, a way-
    ward, sinfu' child;
God's name an' word I didna loe, closed will be
    Heaven's gate—
I wouldna come when Jesus called, an' noo it is
    too late.

"I mind whan I was but a bairn hoo mither aft
    wad speak
O' God's great love an' care for me, an' then
    she'd kiss my cheek,
An' tell me aye to trust in Him, an' He wad be
    my guide ;
But mither dee'd, an' then I strayed far frae the
    Saviour's side.

"Oh ! sir, I mind ae winter nicht, lang years hae
    passed sin' syne,
I gaed wi' mither to the kirk, an', eh ! I thocht
    it fine ;
The music was sae awfu' grand, it a'mast gaur'd
    me greet,
The Bible words the preacher read I thocht sae
    wond'rous sweet.

"I mind his text was frae the Acts ; through a'
    my life sae wild
I've ne'er forgot the words he spoke, though I
    was but a child ;
To find salvation, sir, he said, fowk mony ways
    had tried,
An' yet, ' I am the only way ' the loving Lord
    had cried.

"Salvation will ye no' accept, 'tis offered free
    to a'—
To a', he said, hooever base, wha on the Lord
    will ca';
Sir, could I see him aince again, I'd no' be feared
    to dee,
If I could only hear him say salvation is for me.

"His een were bonnie, bricht, an' blue, his hair
    was like pure gold,
Although it maun be grey lang syne, for he will
    now be old;
His face was like an angel's face, his voice was
    kind an' sweet—
Say, is he deid, or siccan ane, sir, did ye ever
    meet?"

" 'Twas I who preached that sermon, friend, so
    many years ago,
'Twas I who tried the only way to Jesus Christ
    to show;
And this salvation once again is offered free to
    you—
Oh! will you not accept it now, your days on
    earth are few?"

"Oh! what ye say, sir, maun be true, an' yet
  too good it seems
That Christ, to be wi' Him on high, me not
  unworthy deems;
I ken ye wadna tell me wrang, for ane o' His ye
  be—
I'll trust in Him wi' a' my he'rt, an' no' be feared
  to dee."

Christmas Memories.

YES, I know I'm dull and silent,
   But forgive me, friend, to-day,
For my thoughts have crossed the ocean
   To those dear ones far away ;
And while Christmas bells are chiming,
   " Peace on earth, goodwill to men,"
Oh ! they fill my heart with longing
   To see friends and home again.

But between me and my dear ones
   Rolls the wild Atlantic sea,
Yet to-day, although we're parted,
   They'll be thinking all of me ;
And it gives me consolation
   To let fancy sweetly stray
To my home in bonnie Scotland,
   On this holy Christmas Day.

They are gathered all together
  In the cosy sitting-room,
Where the gas has just been lighted
  To shut out the wintry gloom;
And the firelight red is glancing
  On the pictures on the walls,
It upon the oaken cupboard
  And upon the sideboard falls.

By the fire I see my father,   ·
  With his paper in his chair,
His dear face seems graver, older,
  And more thin and white his hair;
In her low chair sits my mother,
  With her knitting on her knee,
Listening to my father reading,
  While their hearts are still with me.

O'er the table bends my sister,
  And a letter she does write;
We together were so happy—
  She and I—last Christmas night;
And I think I hear her saying,
  While her eyes look far away—
" I am writing Harold, mother,
  Have you anything to say ?"

From the piano in the corner
  Comes the sound of music fine,
Jim is playing, while Tom's violin
  Softly joins in "Auld Lang Syne ;"
And my youngest brother's buried
  In some wondrous, thrilling tale
Of adventures in the backwoods,
  Which doth make his cheek turn pale.

Would I could this Christmas evening
  'Mong them in the old room stand,
Hear their dear, familiar voices,
  Kiss each cheek, and clasp each hand.
Vain my wish ; but 'tis sweet comfort,
  Knowing the same God is near,
Watching o'er my dear ones yonder,
  Watching o'er me, lonely here.

The Old Manse.

WRITTEN ON SEEING A PICTURE OF MY OLD HOME.)

THE dear old manse, the dear old manse,
　　'Tis through a mist of tears
This picture of the manse I see,
　My home of childhood's years;
And memory spans the gulf of time,
　And, lo! I am once more
A little boy in big straw hat,
　And holland pinafore.

The old oak tree, the old oak tree,
　The livelong summer day
Beneath its branches on the lawn,
　Beside my nurse, I'd play;
There father sometimes would come out
　To play with me awhile,
And when I laughed he'd kiss my cheek,
　Or pat my head and smile.

Close to the manse the churchyard lay,
 There, in the evening light,
I'd see my father standing oft
 Beside a cross so white;
" Why does he go there, nurse?" I'd ask;
 She'd look at me and sigh—
" Your mother's name is on that stone,
 But she is in the sky."

Into the study I would steal
 When father was not there,
And gaze upon the picture hung
 Above his arm-chair;
For it was mother, and, nurse said,
 It was so like her, too,
And I'd stretch out my hands, and cry—
 "Come back, dear mother, do!"

For she had died when I was born,
 And I had never known
A mother's love, a mother's care,
 A mother of my own.
In vain I'd ask her to come back,
 For that could never be,
But still the picture on the wall
 Would somehow comfort me.

For her dear face was very kind,
    And beautiful to see,
And her soft, tender, hazel eyes
    Seemed smiling down on me ;
And then, nurse said, if I were good
    We'd meet again once more,
For mother, dearest, was not dead,
    But only gone before.

But other faces in the manse,
    Were I there now, I'd see,
And others play upon the lawn,
    Beneath the old oak tree ;
And father's name is on the cross,
    And mother dear and he
Are one again—soon with them, too,
    In Heaven I long to be.

Gerard and I.

WE stood by the stream in the sunlight clear,
  Gerard and I,
Soft cooed the doves in the firwood near,
  Blue was the sky;
Something like this Gerard said to me,
Bending, my blushing face better to see—
   "Darling, be mine,
   I'm only thine;
Thou art dearer than all else on earth to me."

He stood and waited to hear my reply;
  What could I say?
I gave him my hand, and said—"Good-bye;
  Please go away."
But he held it fast, and he did not go,
And from the firwood came, soft and low—
   "He's good and true;
   Accept him—do!"
'Twas only the doves, but they seemed to know.

N

" Answer me, dear one !"—I turned away,
  And would not speak ;
I thought—all right is that word "obey "
  For maidens *meek* ;
To obey *any* man would never suit me—
I'm free just now, and mean so to be.
    " Love makes *all* sweet !"
   The stream at my feet
Seemed to sing, as it rushed to join the sea.

I turned to Gerard, intending to say—
   " It cannot be !"
The look in his eyes made the words die away,
  And thus, you see,
I had to say " Yes," for I could not say " No "—
It seemed too cruel to vex him so.
    " You've done a wise thing,"
   The stream did sing ;
And so cooed the doves, for they seemed to
 know.

In the Mission Hall.

SEE how in crowds they come
From many a darksome slum,
Many a den ;
Women grown hard and bold
In sin's paths, tried and old ;
Wild, vicious men.

Why do they crowd to-night
Into this room so bright,
In from the street ?
There is no whisky here,
No gin their hearts to cheer,
No one to " treat."

What do they come to hear ?
Why, without jest or sneer,
Without a row,
Do they sit silent here ?
Soon all to me is clear—
" 'Ere's parson now !"

Says a rough man to me—
" That's 'im o'er there, ye see ;
  'E's good an' wise ;
'Is heart is kind an' true,
An', whate'er wrong we do,
  'E don't despise ;

" But looks at us so sad
That makes a man feel bad,
  And thus, ye see,
We like to see 'im bright,
So try to do the right,
  Though 'ard it be.

" Hush ! now you'll hear him speak !"
On my companion's cheek
  I see a tear.
What is the charm, I think,
Which can from streets and drink
  Draw these folks here ?

Earnest the words he speaks,
As sin-sick souls he seeks
  For Christ to gain—
" Why will ye thus delay ?
Jesus has washed away
  Every sin stain.

"Come to the Saviour, mates,
To welcome all He waits,
    Come, friends, to-night ;
Give up your evil ways,
Spend all your future days
    As in His sight.

" He wants no offering,
Nothing He'd have you bring,
    Come as you are ;
No good will He withhold,
Though from His blessed fold
    You've wandered far."

And, as he still speaks on,
All former doubts are gone,
    And now I *know*
What brings those rough folks here
What makes the softening tear
    From tired eyes flow.

His is no west-end charge—
Only a parish large,
    'Mong sinful, vile ;
All day he earnest works,
Never a duty shirks—
    Works with a smile.

Sowing the precious seed,
Uprooting every weed,
    He works so hard
Striving sad ones to cheer,
Bringing salvation near ;
    What his reward ?

Enough if from paths of sin
He can the fold within
    Erring ones take ;
Happy if he each day
Something can do or say
    For Jesus' sake.

In Dreamland.

WHEN do I see him whom I loved too well?
  Who called me oft his "darling, bonnie
Nell,"
Who cast me down from Heaven to lowest Hell?
    In dreamland.

His kisses on my cheek when do I feel?
His arm round me again when does it steal?
When do I find him noble, faithful, leal?
      In dreamland.

When do I see the home I left for him?
That bonnie spot beneath the mountain grim,
My father, mother, shepherd lover, Jim?
      In dreamland.

When do Jim's loving words reproach me sore?
My punishment is great, must I bear more?
I see Jim drowned, brought to my father's door,
      In dreamland.

When do I feel once more that maddening joy
That did my better self and thoughts destroy,
Until he cast me off, as child its toy?
        In dreamland.

When do I hunger, pain, and grief forget?
When with repentant tears my pillow wet?
When am I once again my father's pet?
        In dreamland.

When do I clasp my darling mother's hand?
Or in the arbour with my father stand,
The happiest, brightest lass in all the land?
        In dreamland.

So vile am I, my soul so stained with sin,
I can't return again to kith and kin,
I'll only stand my bonnie home within,
        In dreamland.

Where did I read, in happy days of yore,
Of sinful woman brought the Lord before?
Where did I hear those words—"Go, sin no
    more,"
        In dreamland?

No! men may shun with horror those who fall,
But there is One will hear the sinner's call,
And He will save me, for He died for all
      Contrite ones.

So vile am I, and yet I hear Him say—
"Come unto Me, oh! why will you delay?
My blood has washed your every stain away;
      Come, sinner."

"Yea, Lord, I come, a wand'ring, wayward sheep?
The path of virtue may be hard and steep;
Strengthened by Thee, that path I now shall keep
      For ever."

Bidin' His Time.

I'M weary, sae weary o' earth, just bidin' the
Maister's ca';
I ken it canna be lang, for yestreen I was eichty-
twa;
I lang to be wi' Him at rest, freed frae grim
hunger an' cauld,
Safe in yon bricht gowden land, safe in the Guid
Shepherd's fauld.

My freends are a' safe in yon land; lang, lang
I've lived here my lane:
I'd been a wife but sax years whan my guidman
frae me was taen;
I watched him ae winter morn gang oot in his
boatie to sea;
God alane kens whaur he was lost; he never
cam' back to me.

As I grat for my dear guidman oor bairnie crept
    to my knee ;
" Oh, dinna greet sae ! mither dear, whan I'm big
    I'll work for thee ;
Oor Faither in Heaven will be kind to you an'
    me, mither dear ;
He feeds the birds an' the beasts, sae we twa
    hae naething to fear.",

Years passed, an' my laddie grew big ; I asked
    him what he wad be ;
My he'rt grew wae as my Tam chose, like his puir
    faither, the sea ;
I see him yet as he stood on the deck that fair
    summer night,
Kissing his hand to me, wi' the tears in his een
    shinin' bricht.

Sic letters my laddie wrote aboot the places he
    saw,
He tell't me he'd grown sae tall, I wadna ken him
    ava ;
He said he'd be wi' me again afore the end o' the
    year ;
" We'll gang to the kirk thegither on Christmas
    Day, mither dear."

But Christmas Day when it cam' brocht naething
 but sorrow to me,
My laddie was then i' his grave, aneath the cruel
 blue sea;
I sabbed as I heard the sweet bells ring oot on
 the frosty air;
"I canna bide here a' my lane, oh! tak' me,
 Lord, ower there!"

He answered my sorrowfu' cry, but in his ain
 time an' way—
He didna tak' me frae earth, but wark for
 Him gae me to dae;
Noo, in the e'en o' life I'm gaun to thae twa
 lost lang syne—
Ower there, in the Maister's Hame, my jewels
 I'll ne'er again tyne.